A Punch from the Stars

Graeme Goldsmith

A Punch from the Stars

Graeme
Goldsmith

First Published – 2025
This edition published 2025 by Graeme Goldsmith
Brisbane, Qld Australia

The National Library of Australia Cataloguing-in-Publication

Creator: Goldsmith, Graeme, author.

Title: *A Punch from the Stars* / Graeme Goldsmith.

ISBN: 978-1-7642837-0-0 (paperback)

Subjects: Dystopian fiction.
General fiction.
Australian fiction.
Speculative fiction.

This book is a work of fiction and, except in the case of historical fact, any resemblance to actual persons, living or dead, is purely coincidental.

I acknowledge the Traditional Owners and their custodianship of country throughout Australia. I pay my respects to their Ancestors and their descendants, who continue cultural and spiritual connections to Country. I recognise their valuable contributions to Australian and global society.

Typeset in Times New Roman 12pt Donna Munro Graphic Design
Cover image Copyright © 2025 Gloria Le brocq Butler
Printed and bound in Australia by Ingram Spark.

Chapter One

"Hey, Kat, the vice president of the World Ornithological Society just phoned. He's saying no cull. Definitely, no cull."

Katrina Ingledew tugged at the zipper on her red puffer jacket.

"What?" But we have to cull. These emperors are not just massing, they're taking over the whole island."

She gazed out over the seething throng of huddled penguins. Like a sea of rocks covering an endless beach. "I'm worried about our other resident species missing out on their food. Did you tell him about my concerns?"

Dario froze at the doggedness in his fellow scientist's voice. He stood, lost for words.

"Listen," said Kat, continuing to voice her unease, "the only other penguins our drones are spotting are the king, and they're few and far between. Those office-bound idiots in New York aren't here on the ground to witness the crisis we're facing."

"Hey, and I'm telling you what The Society's policy is. They said, no cull."

"But what we're witnessing is a disaster. I'm guessing whole species might have been wiped out. I'm going to have to go higher."

"Higher? But who's higher? And don't forget, this part of Antarctica's a world heritage protection area."

"Well, our drones aren't wrong. I've been studying the footage again and again. I'm telling you, the emperor population has exploded. There's nothing in recorded history to compare with what's going on down here. And they usually only huddle this close in winter."

Dario picked up on the determination in Kat's voice. "Well … you'd better hope you're right … but—"

"Right! Damn it, I know I'm right. I'm getting my gun out and coming back. Got to do something. What we're facing here is the extinction of other penguin species. You coming back too?"

He pulled a face. "I won't be bringing my gun. I don't do killing protected birds."

The early autumn sun dazzled low in a cloudless Antarctic sky, as Katrina and Dario's overstretched shadows traversed the rocky shingle outside the door of the station. As they turned the corner of the building, they both squawked out a cry of disbelief. The swarming emperor hordes had formed an impenetrable mass right up to their quarters. Panic wracked Kat's fur-lined face.

"This is way past crazy," she cried as she scanned the flocking throng of penguins. "Now we're surrounded. These hordes have hemmed us in. They'll be moving into our quarters next."

"Yeah, this is getting scary. How come there's suddenly so many of them?"

"I don't know. Emperors normally stay near the water. I'd like to know how they're getting to the sea to feed."

"You know, Kat, I'm beginning to wonder if that meteorite crash sent them all fleeing here for safety."

"But were there ever as many emperors in the whole of Antarctica?"

Dario lifted his arm to shield his face from the low-hanging sun as he scanned the horizon. The heaving multitude of emperors crowded out as far as the eye could see. His arm fell to his side as he shifted his gaze to the huddle of birds crammed in front of him. He wavered for a moment, his brow furrowed in puzzled observation.

"Hey, Kat. Notice anything different about these little guys here?"

"Yes, they're not as smelly as they usually are."

"No. Take a look at their heads. They're like … bulging. Kind of puffed out. This isn't the normal head profile of the emperor I've come to know."

Kat crouched to check out the nearest birds.

"Whoa! Hey, you're right. It's like… they're deformed or something. Do you think it's a disease, or … I dunno, could they have interbred?"

"Interbred? Oh sure. Interbred with what? What else is there in Antarctica, other than seals and humans?"

Kat raced for the station quarters. She loaded her gun and marched back out.

"Look away if you want Dario, but I'm going to shoot one and take it back for Luke to autopsy."

He covered his ears and turned away as Kat fingered the cold trigger of her rifle. An ear shattering blast boomed out across the frozen Antarctic wilderness.

"This little fellow's nowhere near as heavy as a young emperor should be," said Kat, hauling the lifeless bird over her trim shoulder. "I reckon there's so many now, they're starving. As I said before, how would this little guy have ever got down to the sea through all this mob?"

Once safely back inside their quarters, Kat and Dario headed straight for the lab where she flopped the bird down on the stainless-steel autopsy table.

"I'll go and get Luke. First thing I want him to check out is that weird head bulge—like you said Dario, the enlarged head's not a normal emperor feature." She gazed down and began smoothing the bird's dense black head feathers. "I so want to help save these beautiful birds. Poor things, they must be starving."

Dario shuddered and turned away when he spotted Luke brandishing his handsaw.

"Ooh, I'm going to leave you guys to it." He bolted for the door.

Kat grinned at Luke and shook her head. "Oh, that man, he's such a contradiction. One minute he's the big macho guy. Always acts so tough around me, yet he can't bear to stay and watch a little autopsy."

After Luke completed the dissection, Kat headed out to search for Dario. She wanted her fellow ornithologist's opinion on the result of the extraordinary autopsy discovery. When she found him deeply immersed in phone conversation, she stood, fidgeting with impatience, waiting for his call to end. When he finally hung up, she pounced.

"Got something incredible to tell you—"

"Hey, and I've got something even more incredible to tell you. Oh, go on then—you first."

"The brain of the penguin Luke just dissected: would you believe it's almost a quarter the size again of a normal emperor's brain? I don't know what the hell to make of it."

"Well, that was a call from headquarters over on the mainland. They said our supply plane has just turned back. The emperors have invaded our runway. It's choked with penguins."

Kat gasped. "What? You mean we can't even get our supplies in?" She rolled her eyes, contemplating the worst. "Oh no. That means we can't escape the island. And don't forget, Franklin Island Station was never built to withstand an Antarctic winter."

"Oh Kat. Don't be such a worrywart. Autumn will be with us for a while yet."

"Hey, at these latitudes, winter conditions can start tomorrow. I've experienced abrupt season changes before." She clicked her fingers. "Yeah, just like that."

They both turned their heads as a strange knocking sound came echoing down the hallway from the front entry.

"Who the hell's that?" said Kat. "I thought you said the supply plane wasn't able to land."

She raced to answer the door and gasped in horror. A mob of starving emperors were ravenously pecking wooden strips from the front door of their quarters.

Chapter Two

"Push it up. Right up. Harder, harder." Kat barked out her instructions to graduate scientists, Ross, and Lincoln, as they manhandled a heavy floor-to-ceiling filing cabinet hard up against the station's front door. After their mammoth effort, Ross and Lincoln smirked at each other. Kat took a step back to check on the degree of protection the hulking cabinet afforded. She caught them sniggering at what they fancied to be her erotic vocalisations. "What's so funny, guys?" she enquired, primping her hair. Their raunchy innuendo over her clamourous instructions had gone right over her head.

"No, guys. It's not just the emperors I'm worried about, it's also the force of the wind. Can you restock the cabinet for me now, please? I want to make it as heavy as possible, then I'll get you to fetch another one. Can't take any chances with the fierce winds we get down here."

Ross shot a stupid grin at Lincoln, despite knowing his mate's lust for their older and very vivacious leader was way beyond professional.

At that moment, Dario walked in. How would he have ever known Kat's prediction about the polar autumn turning to winter would come to haunt them. Just two days after raising her fears, the weather lurched from sunny skies to freezing blizzards. This was Kat's third stint on Franklin Island. She'd experienced it all before. She had more knowledge than any of them and knew now was the time the entire team should be evacuating their summer quarters.

Dario did a double take at the hulking filing cabinet blockading the entry. "So, what's all this about?"

"Can't take any chances with wind, Dario. The emperors are hell bent on destroying the front door. We'd all end up dying of hypothermia if I didn't take some action."

"And what about an escape exit if a fire breaks out? Bet you didn't think of that, did you?"

"Oh, for goodness sakes," she said, placing her hands on her shapely hips. "You know what? I'm so over your constant negativity. I'm the team leader here, and I'm doing my best to keep us all safe. What else do you expect me to do, given the circumstances we're facing?"

Apart from the deterioration in the weather, the other concern for the team at Franklin Station was the besieging of both the building and the aircraft runway by the swarming emperor hordes. The team reeled in horror as the birds continued their freakish destruction of the wood on the sturdy entrance door. But it was the shock of witnessing the first splinter of daylight coming through the door that had mobilised Kat into breakneck fortification measures.

After Kat and the boys completed their task of securing the entrance, they headed to the staff cafeteria. With its extensive timber table and casual leather sofas bordering the walls, the station cafeteria endowed the team with a much-needed social outlet—an opportunity to bounce ideas and exchange scientific theories.

"I don't know what we're going to do about getting out of this place." Kat slumped down with the others at the table. Today, her immaculately made-up face was creased with worry.

"But the weather will get back to normal. Won't it?" asked Dario.

"We can hope. But sometimes, when a winter pattern sets in early, it doesn't budge till spring. And with the emperors taking over the runway, we're completely cut off. I mean, they're everywhere—from our front door, right down to the sea. It's beyond crazy."

"Have to kill them off then. Kapow," said Ross simulating a trigger with his finger.

"Can't do that, *boy*," Dario snorted. "Emperors are a protected species. And even if we did get permission, we don't have the ammunition."

"Well, looks like we'll just have to ride it out till spring," said Lincoln, his frisky eyes ogling Kat.

She flinched at his immature boorishness, wriggling uncomfortably in her chair. Being the only female in an all-male team wasn't easy for Kat. Especially having to endure the constant unwanted attention of two testosterone-fuelled graduates. Although she'd acquired competence in martial arts, she knew she'd be no match for the youthful likes of Lincoln or Ross.

"Hey guys, some good news." Matt, the electronics engineer bounced in excitedly. "Headquarters are sending in a helicopter with the supplies the plane couldn't deliver."

"Supplies?" Kat scowled. "Hah, they should be coming to rescue us. We can't even get out the front door for emperors. And look how the weather's turned."

"Yeah," said Dario glaring at Kat. "The sooner we get out of this hellhole the better."

"I agree. I'll get a refrigerated carrier ready for the autopsied emperor brain. I've been ordered to have it airfreighted straight to the Ornithological Society in the United States."

"And what the hell are they going to do with it?"

Kat rolled her eyes. "My thoughts exactly, Dario. Please don't tell anyone, but I'm arranging for a second one to be airfreighted to my scientist friend Hugo Schuster, in the UK. He's been studying Avian viruses for some time now."

Chapter Three

The next morning on Franklin Island dawned steely grey. The gusty winds had eased a little. Kat took an early call from headquarters informing her the helicopter was in the process of being refuelled and loaded with supplies. Estimated time of arrival at the station was scheduled for midday. Although she pleaded her case for rescue, she was advised a decision of that importance would have to come from a higher authority.

Kat and the team met soon after headquarters had contacted, in order to work out a plan for transferring the supplies from the helicopter into the emperor-besieged station.

"Time we got rid of those ridiculous filing cabinets, and opened the front door," said Dario, attempting to garner support from the guys.

"No," cried Kat. "The cabinets will remain in place until the helicopter has safely landed. Those winds out there are still gusting twenty-five knots. What if the helicopter can't land? Anyway, we probably don't have a front door anymore."

After Kat asserted her authority, and considered some fervent debate, she ordered the team to the eastern portal window to observe the landing. She maintained that only once the chopper had landed would the door be cleared of the two protective cabinets.

Half an hour before midday, Kat ordered the rugged steel shutter of the eastern portal window be raised. The crude clattering of the shutter mechanism left the long rectangular shaped triple glazed window exposed for full view of the helipad.

As the team stood huddled at the window, a waft of hot breath steamed Kat's long and elegant neck. She spun around to find Lincoln brazenly nestled in behind her. Although his lanky body wasn't quite in physical contact, she recoiled at the affront of his encroachment.

"Lincoln! do you have to breathe down my neck?"

"Eh? Oh…oh, sorry, I wasn't aware I was."

Ross sniggered in the background, then muttered, "hey, good try there, Linc, ol' boy."

The ruttish behaviour of the young graduates made Kat even more determined to vacate the artificial confinement of the summer station and return to normal society. She barged her way forward taking up premiere position right in front of the window.

By 12:10 p.m. Kat was squirming with impatience.

"Where the hell are they? I can't make out a thing on this murky horizon. Can you guys see any sign of them yet?"

A chorus of 'nos' echoed from behind.

"Just hope the chopper's big and ugly enough to scare off the emperors, otherwise our supplies won't be landing this time either," said Lincoln."

Kat turned to face him. "So, tell me, Lincoln. Would you stay on a helipad with all that commotion and turbulence coming at you from above?"

"Nope. But I'm not a dumb emperor, am I."

"Smart b——, " Kat mumbled under her breath.

"Hey! I can see it. Here it comes," shouted Ross. His youthful eyes had picked up a tiny speck on the distant horizon.

"Yeah, he's right. It's coming into view. Look, look. There it is," said Lincoln angling his head toward the welcome sight.

"Oh yes, I can see it now." Kat let out an excited giggle. "What a relief. I've so been missing my morning turmeric detoxes."

There was more sniggering from behind. A rumour had been circulating around the station, that when home in Sydney, Kat was so body-obsessive, she kept a list of all the local gyms remaining open on Christmas Day.

"They're getting close. Don't you reckon it's time to get those filing cabinets away from the entrance?" Dario ranted, in another attempt to get everyone on side.

Kat scowled and swung around to quash his remark. "I will be the one to make that decision, thank you, Dario."

The helicopter zoomed into full view. Never had the Franklin team been so excited about their supplies being replenished. With their basic foodstuffs almost exhausted, a spirited buzz of relief filled the air.

As the chopper bore down on the landing pad, the anticipated emperor withdrawal wasn't happening.

"Oh, those crazy birds." Dario cried. "What? Are they suicidal or something?"

Everyone stared in astonishment as the emperors began raising their beaks in the air, audaciously trying to attack the gigantic roaring bird above. Then without warning, a blast of flames exploded out from beneath the helicopter. In a flash, the doomed chopper plummeted to the ground, crumpling into a blazing fireball right before their eyes.

"Nooo! Nooo!" Kat wailed, "They'll be killed, they'll all be killed."

A deathly silence hung in the air as the horror of the disaster sank in.

"What…? What went wrong?" Dario whimpered, shaking his head. "I can't… I don't understand."

"Unbelievable," cried Matt, his mouth gaping open. "I'll contact headquarters. Get a rescue team out."

"Yes, yes, please do, Matty," said Kat staring into his moist eyes.

It appeared very obvious the pilot, and his co-pilot, wouldn't have stood a hell's chance of surviving an inferno of such flaming intensity. A fleeting flash of Tom, the forever smiling guy who'd have been piloting the chopper, flickered in Kat's head. Tears welled as she pictured his handsome face, and the scenic joyrides he'd indulged her during last season's stint in Antarctica.

Without uttering a word, Kat bumbled her way past the shellshocked team and dashed to her room. In a rage of blubbering agony, she punched her pillow with such fury, the seam split, and a pall of downy feathers exploded into the air.

Chapter Four

When Kat finally emerged from the refuge of her room, she was welcomed by a warm and enveloping hug from Matt. He took a step back to give her the once over. His eyes were still watery. His brow furrowed with concern over how she might be coping with the horror of the chopper disaster. After Kat reassured the station's gentle giant she was okay, he related some depressing news: there was to be no mission to recover the victims of the helicopter crash. He moved on to explain this wasn't because of the unlikelihood of any survivors, but because no other air services were available at mainland headquarters.

"And what about the supplies we so desperately need?" she pleaded.

"Well, as you know, a plane can't land, and there's no more choppers. We really are stranded. Totally isolated. The only reassuring news is the crash made world headlines, so maybe something can be worked out."

Kat scowled up to his stern frown. "Hah, not much good us making world headlines, Matty—not if we all end up starving to death."

"I'm sure there'll be an international push for us to be rescued."

He reached down and placed his hand on her shoulder. "Anyway, don't worry, we won't starve. Plenty of birds out there to eat."

She pulled a face. "Please tell me you're joking," she cried, with a squirming shudder.

"No. I kid you not. It wouldn't be the first-time penguin meat's been on the menu. I remember from my student days, how the old Antarctic explorers, and even the early sailors, all indulged in penguin meat when they had to."

After observing Kat's impassioned dash from the viewing area after the crash, Matt deliberately avoided mentioning the chopper victims. He sensed she must have known either the pilot or co-pilot.

Matt also refrained from telling Kat the initial news report on the crash had attracted an avalanche of controversy. The big-league US television reporter who first broke the story had tactlessly discounted the seriousness of the crash by chuckling about how the Antarctic team were *'being held hostage by a gang of penguins at the bottom of the world.'* The reporter's jesting remark was widely criticised as being in bad taste. The aftermath of his inadvertent wisecrack had seen him temporarily stood down from his revered position.

On the morning after the helicopter crash, Dario deployed his beloved drone to record footage of the wreckage site. On its return, he was stunned to find the emperors were already back, huddled right up to the burned-out chopper. Even more puzzling was the lack of any evidence of dead or injured penguins at the scene of the fiery explosion.

After delivering his bizarre findings to Kat, she told Dario she'd call a team meeting for

2 p.m. Her aim was to brainstorm ideas on how they might work together to solve their pressing dilemma.

"Anyway," she said, checking her watch. "I'm off now to the gym, Dario. I'll see you at 2 p.m."

Later, after a strenuous workout, and just before she was about to start her meeting, Kat took an unexpected call from headquarters. When she finally walked into the cafeteria, she froze in disbelief: the meeting had already commenced without her. There was Dario, out front, in the throes of wowing the guys with images of his drone surveillance footage. He then asked the team for their thoughts on why there appeared to be no sign of any emperor deaths on the runway. From his commanding position, he cast Kat a smirking glance, obviously revelling in the fact he'd succeeded in spawning such a lively flood of discussion.

Kat hovered at the back of the room, her face fuming red at having her meeting hijacked by the ever-bumptious Dario. She grated a chair across the floor and plonked herself down. *Bastard. He's made a fool of me again. I'll get him for this.*

Kat kept her head bowed, attempting to avoid Dario's beaming face. Out of nowhere something snapped inside. In a sudden outburst of exasperation, she rose from her seat and stormed out. She headed for her room, wrenched open the drawers of her bedside table and rummaged for her last box of cream-centred chocolates. In a pique of anger and humiliation, she lay back on the bed and in one reckless lapse, wolfed down the entire pack.

Chapter Five

On the third floor of the administrative centre of the World Ornithological Society in New York, President Levi Stanton, and his deputy, Henri Dubois, were meeting to discuss recent reports about the strange clustering of emperor penguins in Antarctica.

Tension hung in the air. Henri, one of the Society's career-driven generation of upcoming go-getters, was aching to take the reins from Levi, who, at the age of sixty-eight, was only just contemplating retirement. Henri, himself, was already greying, but Levi, two decades his senior, still retained a head of thick jet-black hair, a perfectly trimmed black moustache, and flawless olive skin.

"Ah, Henri, good to see you again," Levi took his hand in both of his. "Take a seat my man; I'm itching to hear about your adventures. You sure look as though you've been living it up in sunnier climes." He let out a chuckle. "I can see the white patches where your sunnies have been. But before we get onto your time in New Guinea, tell me, were you able to keep up with all the news coming out of Antarctica?"

"Yes, I was. I had access to news reports every day."

"Don't you think it's bizarre, what's going on down there with the penguins in the Antarctic? The Franklin team have kept me updated with their latest drone footage. The emperors' behaviour really is something else. Hang on," he said, skating his chair over the plush carpet like some exuberant schoolboy, "have a look at the footage I received this morning."

With the click of his remote, Levi played the latest drone recording on his wide-screen video and sat back.

"Can you believe this?" he clamoured as the scene opened.

Henri sat in wide-eyed astonishment, gaping at the unending sea of emperor penguins encircling the station on Franklin Island.

"Weird, isn't it?" said Levi, straightening his tie. "Never seen anything like it before. I had one of our local ornithologists check the last surveyed populations of emperor penguins. There's nothing in recorded history to compare with the massing they're doing there right now."

He stopped the video and looked Henri straight in the eye. "I want a rescue operation organised. And fast. The team down there are being held virtual prisoners, and we need to find out what the hell's going on with those birds."

"But shouldn't the Australians be sorting things out for themselves?" Henri griped. "Why should we always be the ones to bail out the rest of the world? Our funding's too hard-earned to keep doing it over and over."

"Hmm, I don't agree, Henri. Don't forget my good friend and colleague Katrina Ingledew, is stranded on the island. Kat would have to be one of the world's leading ornithologists. I'm hoping she'll join our team here one day." He paused and gazed out the window. "Yes, it's no wonder she never married. I know first-hand how she's dedicated her life to researching Antarctic birds. No. We must do something to help her."

Levi insisted, that as the world's leading ornithological authority, they must be seen to be leading the way.

When Levi described his deputy's recent conservation mission to New Guinea as 'paling to insignificance' compared to the situation in Antarctica, Henri's smouldering face glowed an even deeper red. He sat, tapping his fingers on the leather armrests, avoiding Levi's gaze.

"Anyway, Henri, what do you make of their claim there's been a change in the shape of the emperor's heads?"

Henri grunted. His eyes scanned the room. He'd already surmised what Levi was up to. *This man's planning to retire on a high. He wants to make this rescue mission the pinnacle of his career—to go out leaving a lasting personal legacy.*

Levi pretended not to notice Henri's annoyance. "Well, I can tell you, the change in their head shape has me stumped. Did you know a brain sample from an autopsy was to have been placed aboard the ill-fated helicopter?" He leaned back in his chair. "Hmm, all very puzzling. Anyway, I'm getting a team together. Have to get down there—find out for ourselves. You interested in joining us?"

Despite a tentative thumbs down response from his deputy, and with the harsh Southern Hemisphere winter approaching, time was running out. Levi ploughed full steam ahead, implementing an immediate mobilization for a combined rescue and investigative mission to Antarctica.

The newly formed rescue team concluded their own South Pole research base would prove their most dependable access point. It was also the only outpost guaranteed to provide a full range of suitable rescue helicopters. Their plan was to avoid attempting another risky helicopter landing. It had been decided they'd simply hover over the entrance of the station and winch each person up one at a time.

Under Levi's seasoned leadership, the mission was expected to be ready for deployment in just seven days.

As late as day five, Henri still hadn't given Levi a definite yes or no as to whether he'd be joining the mission. The way his plea to conserve the society's precious funding had been rejected by Levi, left him wallowing in a black hole of resentment. He phoned into work every day, 'sick.' But after each call he crashed back into bed reeling with panicky self-doubts about his emotional state of mind.

While it riled Henri his non-participation in the team wouldn't worry Levi in the slightest, it bugged him his boss might, singlehandedly, get to bathe in the glory of their organisation's heroic rescue.

Highlighting the urgency of the planned rescue, and only days before the team were due to leave on their Antarctic mission, Levi received news the Franklin Island team had been forced to resort to eating penguin meat to survive.

Chapter Six

Just two days before the departure of the Ornithological Society's polar rescue mission, the initially reluctant Henri, finally made the decision to join the team. After wallowing in a mire of anxiety and broody ruminating, he came to the realization that if he was ever going to take over the reins of The Society, he needed to be right up there supporting their current agenda. His last-minute change of heart was welcomed by Levi, who fast tracked arrangements for his travel.

Levi Stanton, and his deputy Henri Dubois, relaxed back in luxurious business class seats as their commercial flight to Christchurch, New Zealand, zoomed over the international dateline and on into the setting sun. Despite his initial protest at the unnecessary expense of flying business class, he was overruled by Levi. Once again, Henri concluded, that with his long-awaited retirement looming, Levi was determined to make the most of his position and indulge in as much privilege as possible during the closing chapter of his celebrated career.

A few glasses of wine armed Henri with the courage to tackle Levi over what he viewed as his reckless spending on business class seats.

"Anyway, what are we doing here in business class?" he asked, as he swigged yet another mouthful of premium red wine.

"What do you mean?"

"Why is it the rescue team are back there in economy while you and I are sitting here in the lap of luxury."

Levi fiddled with his starched napkin. He didn't reply.

"Well, I see all this," Henri put down his glass, "as squandering The Society's funds. It's indulgent and it's wasteful. We should all be travelling together as a team. Sorry Levi, but I'm going to raise the question of this unnecessary spending at the AGM when we get home."

Levi bowed his head and toyed with his cuff links. Not another word was spoken. Henri slouched back and fell into a wine-woozy slumber.

A bonging turbulence chime snapped Henri from his doze. His head had slumped toward Levi's seat. But when he opened his eyes, the seat was empty. Another chime rang out. He sat up to see his boss stumbling back to his seat. The minute Levi sat down, he began writhing and rubbing his hands over his chest.

"Ooh, don't know what I've eaten, but I'm in terrible pain."

"My guess is indigestion. That's the price you pay for excess. If we'd travelled economy like the rest of the team, you'd be fine."

After a brief transfer flight from Auckland and their eventual arrival in Christchurch, the weary team were whisked straight to their five-star airport hotel for a late dinner and a good night's sleep in preparation for their early flight to Antarctica next day.

Henri jumped out of bed at 4 a.m. next morning, refreshed and ready for an eagerly anticipated a la carte breakfast. However, he recoiled at the face staring back at him in the steamy bathroom mirror. His recent bout of despair had all but killed his appetite. His travel weary face appeared hollow-cheeked and drawn. He ran is fingers through his hair, positive it had turned even greyer.

"Got to eat big this morning," he muttered. "Make up for the weight I lost while I was down in the dumps."

With fresh resolve, he headed out of his room toward the lobby and the hotel restaurant. As he turned the corner from the accommodation wing, he was greeted by a flurry of activity. Two uniformed paramedics wheeling an empty stretcher trolley flew past him. They were speeding back in the direction from where he'd just emerged.

Oh no, someone must be in trouble. He eyed the signage pointing out the direction of the restaurant.

"Morning Sir," an impeccably presented young waitress addressed him at the restaurant door. "May I have your room number please?"

"Ah … oh, I'm with the United States Antarctic rescue team, I believe we're all sitting together."

The waitress gestured to a large round table, all elegantly set out on white linen, but with no one seated.

"Strange," Henri muttered. *And here I was thinking I was running late.*

The waitress and Henri spun around as one of the reception staff's squeaky heels approached from behind.

"Just letting you know," the receptionist whispered to the waitress, "looks as though one of the guests from the US delegation is being rushed off to hospital. I'm wondering if their team will make it to breakfast."

Henri jumped on hearing the words, 'US delegation.' "Excuse me, I'm one of those guests. I'm surprised I'm the only one here."

"Oh… sorry sir, but I'm afraid a member of your group is being attended to by an ambulance crew. You may want to go and find out more." She pointed to the accommodation wing.

Henri recalled the two paramedics with an empty stretcher trolley racing down the hallway. He dashed off. As he turned the corner, he recognized the face of one of his team huddled at a suite doorway and ran towards him.

"What's happened?" he enquired, puffing out his words.

"It's Professor Stanton," said Kyle, the team's Emergency Response Officer, removing his glasses and shaking his head. "The paramedics think he's had a heart attack. There's an ambulance outside waiting to take him to a hospital."

They all stood back as the paramedics wheeled Levi to the door. Henri gasped as he caught a glimpse of his leader's ashen face. His body appeared lifeless.

No, no, not Levi. How can this be? Levi, who's always been so young and fit for his age. The seriousness of the moment suddenly overcame him. *Oh no, and I dismissed his pain as indigestion on the flight over.*

Henri trembled inside. He steadied himself against the wall as the paramedics wheeled Levi away. *The team's flight to the US Base is scheduled for take-off in just three hours. Who's going to lead our rescue mission now? Looks like I'm it. I'm going to have to make some major decisions. And right away.*

After much deliberation and a message of endorsement from The Society's secretary in New York, Henri accepted the planned rescue must go ahead with him leading the operation. Levi's wife would catch the first plane out to be with him, and the team would still fly out, as scheduled, at 7 a.m.

If I'm ever going to take over as Society president, this is my best shot at proving I'm up to the job.

As they waited to board their Antarctic flight at Christchurch airport, Henri received a puzzling message from head office. An international news report had come in about a group of locals in the sub-Antarctic region of Tierra del Fuego. The reporter stated the locals were sitting on a beach encircled by a massing throng of king penguins. Although unsubstantiated, the Chilean reporter claimed the penguins appeared fixated on staring up to the sky.

Chapter Seven

After take-off from Christchurch airport, Henri turned in his seat, craning his neck to take in his first ever glimpse of Southern Hemisphere snow. The aircraft climbed rapidly to showcase the majesty of New Zealand's snow-capped Southern Alps.

The Society's Emergency Response Officer, Kyle, chose to sit next to Henri. As soon as a blanket of dazzling white cloud began obscuring their vision, the two commenced discussing the complexities of the rescue mission they were about to undertake.

"So … what are your plans for the operation?" Henri enquired.

Kyle shut the window blind and swapped his sunnies for his usual glasses. "From what we've learned, we'll have to fly the chopper in and hover above the entrance to Franklin Station. I've done similar rescues before, and I can tell you, it's no easy feat. An air rescue can be a terrifying ordeal for those on the ground."

"I could never do what you do, Kyle. I'm an office-bound sort of guy. It would scare the pants off me, even being rescued."

"Yeah, I'll be going down to reassure each one of them. And I'll ensure they're all safely harnessed before being winched up and brought aboard the chopper."

Henri flinched. He turned his eyes to the floor. *Wow, how brave is this young guy? And what the hell am I doing here? Management people like me can't do a thing to help.*

Having commenced his career in finance, Henri knew the Society owed its existence to the generosity of community donations and the occasional bequest. He still couldn't reconcile himself to the recent excesses of Levi's tenure, especially the extravagance of splashing out on business class airfares. *Yes, there's going to be some big changes when I take over as president.*

For the remainder of the six-hour flight, Kyle fell into a pattern of brief chatter and longer periods of snoozing. Henri was writhing with indigestion, after gulping down his hotel breakfast. His stomach had commenced somersaulting after Levi's deathly white body was wheeled past him on the way to the waiting ambulance. And now, hours later, he was still paying the price. He had to wonder if his discomfort was payback for his lack of sympathy for Levi on their flight to Christchurch.

The first thing Henri observed as he set foot on terra polar was how low the sun hung on the horizon. He gawked at the ground staff's overstretched shadows. Despite a cloudless sky, the weak low-slung sun imparted an eerie absence of warmth. *Yes, about the same warmth as the moon,* he thought to himself.

Henri had shivered on his arrival in autumnal Christchurch, but the icy wind here cut his face like a shard off a glacier.

Once inside the US Base, Henri and the team were whisked off to the diner for their first meal. The café's round table provided the team the opportunity to discuss tomorrow's planned rescue. Henri was relieved to hear a suitable helicopter had been fully prepared and everything made ready for Kyle, and the pilot's mid-morning flight to Franklin Island. But apart from providing regular updates to head office, he still had to ask himself *what am I here for?*

After dinner, Henri was briefed on how Franklin Island team leader, Katrina Ingledew, had reported abusive behaviour from a member of her team. During her call for help the previous day, she cited fellow employee, Dario Cross, who'd accused her of plundering more than her fair share of the team's dwindling food supplies. Dario's accusation stemmed from her refusal to eat penguin meat. Kat claimed the man's anger turned so violent, he'd grabbed her by the throat. She added it was only her mastery of martial arts that saved her from his malicious intent.

Henri requested an urgent call to find out exactly what was happening at Franklin Island Station. He wanted reassurance the situation had calmed.

Henri winced as he picked up the phone to call Kat. He was also going to have to tell her the news about her good friend Levi Stanton.

"Hello, Kat? No, I'm not Levi. I'm Levi's deputy, Henri, from New York."

"Oh, I'd been expecting a call. I've been looking forward to seeing him again."

"Ah … yes … listen, Kat, I'm afraid I have some bad news about Levi. Unfortunately, he fell ill while we were staying overnight in Christchurch."

A stony silence ensued.

"Oh. What's happened then?"

Henri went on to explain Levi's condition. He reassured Kat, her friend was being taken good care of in the local hospital and his wife should soon be at his side.

"But I am very concerned about the team morale you have at the station, Kat. Just want to let you know our rescue helicopter will be there around mid-morning tomorrow to get you all out."

"Don't worry. I'm quite okay. These guys should have known better than to mess with me. They're all acting weird—the lot of them. I'm feeling like I'm the only one in touch with reality."

"Well, please let them know we'll be evacuating them tomorrow. I'll be here to meet you at the base when you arrive. Just wanted to let you know about Levi, and check the team are all okay."

The one administrative role to which Henri *did* contribute, was to remind Kat about the importance of bringing a sample from the autopsied penguin brain with her for dispatch to The Society in New York.

The decreasing sunlight hours heralding the Antarctic winter, made the imminent rescue of the Franklin Island team even more pressing. The time was approaching when there'd be no more daylight whatsoever.

Chopper pilot Ben, and rescue man, Kyle, were relieved to wake to a clear calm morning and decided to leave as soon as possible. Henri made sure he was at the departure gate to shake both their hands and wish them a successful operation. As they filed out of the warmth to an icy chill and the waiting helicopter, he lingered in silent observation until the chopper disappeared into the palest of blue horizons.

The base team's anxious wait ended with the hovering chopper relaying the first screen shot of Franklin Island Station.

The deployment of both on-board, and on-body cameras had been prearranged to allow Henri and the team live coverage of the entire proceedings.

"Where are they all then?" Henri cried, as a clear aerial view of the building came into view. Although he spied the ever-present throng of encircling emperors, there was no sign of the team.

"Hey, there's someone now. Look, coming out the front entrance."

" Oh yes, that must be Kat," said Henri bouncing with excitement. "Yes, yes, it must be her. She has a bag strapped to her waist."

They fell silent, waiting for the other members to appear.

"So where are the rest of them?" asked the base team leader, as he observed the live screening.

They stood spellbound as Kyle's head camera recorded his descent down the rescue line. Kat positioned herself to have her harness fitted and the two began their intrepid ascent to the hovering chopper.

"Hey," cried Henri. "What about the others? Why aren't they lining up?"

The cam switched to Kyle's face. "Listen guys," he panted to the camera. "Kat's saying the rest of the team are refusing to be rescued. She's telling me they're all acting weird. She said one even tried to beat her up. She's the only team member who wants to come with us. So, yeah, we're outta here."

'But, but—" Henri's protest was interrupted by the whining thrum of the powerful engine and the camera cutting out.

Chapter Eight

The mechanical chopping of distant helicopter blades alerted Henri of the rescue party's imminent return well before he sighted its landing at the Antarctic base. He ceased his incessant pacing and observed from the warm comfort of the observation window as Kyle and Kat strode their way toward the massive glass doors fronting the building.

The warm welcome Henri had promised Kat, fell flat. She froze in silence as he began raging at Kyle.

"What the hell did you think you were doing, Kyle? Cutting me dead with your camera, then abandoning the rest of the Franklin Island team?"

Kyle's jaw dropped open. "What do you mean?"

"Why didn't you go into the station and check on them? Why didn't you make sure they weren't too frightened to be rescued?"

"Hey now. That was not my role. If you want to perform a check, we'll go back tomorrow. You can go down and negotiate with them yourself. I acted on the information Kat provided at the time. She made it quite clear they didn't want to be rescued. That's the instruction I followed."

Henri snorted and turned to face Kat. "What the hell's been going on at Franklin Island—that none of your team wanted to be rescued?"

"I did tell you on the phone. Remember? I said they were all acting weird."

"Weird? Weird?" His arms waved in the air. "What do you mean by weird?"

"They're in a state of denial—they're almost out of food, and winter's fast approaching. It's like they're all sitting around waiting for something to happen. But for the life of me, I can't figure what. Not one of them would speak to me after Dario tried to strangle me."

"Strangle you! He tried to strangle you," Kyle exclaimed.

"Yes, Dario accused me of using up their food because I refused to eat penguin meat."

"Hell. Now I'm glad I didn't go in to rescue them."

Henri turned to Kat and reached out to shake her hand. "Hello, Kat. I'm Henri, from The Society in New York. You'll have to excuse my rant. It's just, I got so exasperated when the filming cut out."

"Thats okay. But please tell me how Levi's doing?"

"Last I heard, Levi was stable. His wife should be at his bedside by this time. I'll be doing my regular New York conferencing link shortly. I'll get a full run down on his condition."

Kat opened the container on her waistband and handed a canister to Henri. "This is the emperor brain specimen you asked for."

"Hah, sounds like we need a brain specimen from your team members as well," he sneered.

The story about their odd behaviour had him relating the bizarre report he'd received while waiting to board his plane in New York. How a news reporter had claimed that a group of Tierra del Fuegians were sitting on a local beach amidst a throng of King penguins. The reporter had stated, the birds were acting in a puzzling manner, with their eyes fixed to the sky.

Henri frowned as Kat make a sudden lurch for Kyle. She threw her arms around him, momentarily resting her head on his chest. "Thank you so much, Kyle, for getting me out of that hell hole. I've been so frightened. I thought Dario was going to get even with me for embarrassing him in front of the team—you know, with my martial arts skills." She released her embrace and gazed up at him.

Kyle's face blushed red. "No worries. Rescues are what I'm trained to do. Maybe you can teach me some of your martial arts moves one day."

"I'd love to."

"Okay, okay," Henri interrupted their prattle. "I was going to wait for Ben to come in from the tarmac, but c'mon, let's go and get your accommodation sorted eh, Kat."

There were around thirty vacant rooms in the Base's accommodation quarters, but the room Henri had allocated for Kat was right next to his. He led her down the polished concrete hallway, opened the door and turned on the light. "I'm sure you'll be okay in here."

Kat drew a breath. The windowless room was austere. Bare bones basic. One narrow single bed with a beige doona, one wooden side table, and one plastic chair—the kind of room perhaps a man might put up with.

"Must say I'm looking forward to working with you, Kat. Levi's told me so much about your dedication to your career."

She cast her eyes down trying to avoid his lingering gaze. "Yes, there's a lot we need to investigate—about what's happening with the emperors. But first; please, Henri: clothes? toiletries? I have nothing. Oh, and I'll get you to show me where the gym is."

"Of course. I'll get some clothing organised now so you can change and shower before lunch. And by the way, your room's right next to mine if you need me … for anything."

Kat averted her eyes again.

"Come on then, I'll get one of the staff to take you to the stores and get you outfitted."

When it was time for lunch, Kat made a beeline for the empty seat next to Kyle in the staff cafeteria. Henri arrived moments after and sat directly opposite. As he pulled out his chair, she discreetly inched hers back from the table.

"Ah," he said, "all fitted out I see. I was told they were all men's clothes in there, but gee you look good in them."

Kat ignored his remark and began picking at the food on her plate, favouring only the mushy overcooked vegetables.

The casual conversation soon turned to Franklin Island and Henri's preoccupation with rescuing the remaining team.

"So, Kyle, what time tomorrow can we get airborne and get those guys out of there?"

"Roughly the same time as we left this morning, Henri, depending on the light and the weather. And don't worry, I won't carry out my threat to send you down the rescue line." He let out a chuckle. "No. I'll go down and find out whether it's just fear that's stopping them from wanting to be rescued. Anyway, there wouldn't be room for you and all the others on board, so I'll set up the camera for you again. You can view my interaction with them on the big screen. I won't turn it off on you this time. Promise."

"Don't forget, you might have a hefty filing cabinet to budge out of the doorway," said Kat.

"I had it positioned there to keep the emperors out … oh and the pong."

The sun still hadn't risen when Kyle and pilot, Ben sat down with Henri for breakfast the next morning. A few moments later, Kat sauntered in. After tapping a small spoon of steaming porridge onto her plate, she joined them at one of the round tables.

"Sun's coming up so late now," she said as she sidled in next to Kyle. You do realize we're just days away from twenty-four-hour darkness."

"Only days?" exclaimed Henri.

"Yes. The autumn darkness accelerates at an incredibly fast rate. Sunset begins closing in by half an hour a day at these latitudes. It's kind of freakish."

"Hmm, you think that's freakish," said Ben. "Last night's light show was even more spooky."

"The great Aurora Australis, eh?" said Henri.

"No. Definitely not the legendary old 'rora. I've seen that show so many times. No, these were white lights—a bit like blinding car headlights, but high in the sky. The curtains in my room are never closed." He let out a laugh. "Yeah, well there's no one outside to stare in, is there?"

When daylight did eventually dawn at the station, Ben and Kyle ceased their restless pacing and readied themselves for departure. Despite a murky layer of high cloud, they were relieved the breeze remained gentle—nothing that might hamper a tricky rescue operation.

Once again, Henri stood in front of the massive glass doors, shaking their hands before the pair marched out to the waiting helicopter. Kat, meanwhile, chose to remain in the cafeteria. She'd conveyed her goodbyes and wished them well for their mission from her chair in front of the viewing screen. Kyle had already activated the display for the final test.

Secretly, Kat was hoping the Franklin Island guys wouldn't change their minds. Her stomach churned at the prospect of coming face to face with the obnoxious Dario again.

Kat's anxiety over Dario tempered the flinching unease of having Henri join her to view the rescue proceedings. She kept her distance, wary of his overfamiliarity and his clumsy innuendo. His behaviour reminded her of young Lincoln, back at the station. Not something she expected from a man her own age.

Henri and Kat sat glued to the big screen, chorusing their enthusiasm over the stunning Antarctic scenery—the endless expanses of dazzling white, occasionally broken by the shadowy grey of craggy uplands and rocky coastal stretches.

"Nearly there now. I can make out the island already," Ben shouted to Kyle above the chopper's thunderous engines.

"Yep, yep. I can see Franklin now too."

Kat and Henri had no chance of spotting the distant island on their screen. But they both moved in closer, hoping for an aerial view the moment the chopper began hovering over the station.

"There it is. There's the building now," cried Ben. "Hey, you guys, we'll be right overhead in less than a minute," he puffed into the camera.

A few seconds of silence from Ben was broken by an exclamation. "Woah. Woah!" he shouted above the whirring din of the chopper blades. "I don't believe this."

"What the…?" cried Kyle. "They're all dead! The emperors are all fricking dead! It looks like a mass extinction down there."

"Hey guys," cried Ben. "Don't know whether you can view it on your screen, but there's a sea of dead emperors, as far as the eye can see. They're all lying lifeless. Every single emperor. Dead as dodos!"

Chapter Nine

"Hey, Kat," Kyle shouted into the cockpit camera. "I'm thinking—you know, it is only morning. If this penguin extinction happened during the night, and looks as though that was the case, your team inside the Station probably don't even know about it yet."

"You're probably right. There's no sign of them down there," Ben chipped in. "Hey, you 'bout ready to go down now, Kyle? I need to keep an eye on our fuel level."

"Yep, that's what I'm here for. Hang on, Kat, I'll put my head camera on so you can follow all the action." He leaned into the camera. "And Henri, you'll get the message loud and clear if the guys are still refusing to be rescued. I don't want to be the one getting into any scuffles with them."

Kat and Henri sat in silence as Kyle's head camera recorded his speedy descent. He unclipped himself, then dodged his way over the bodies of lifeless emperors on his way to the station entrance.

"I see what you mean about there being some sort of barricade at the door, Kat. Oh, hang on, no, it's not hard up against the door. I'm just about to ease my way in. Yes! just." He panted. "No worries. All okay getting through the door."

Kat breathed a sigh of relief.

"Hello? … Hello? Where are you guys?"

Although the entry was flooded with bright lighting, there was no reply.

"Hello, hello," he kept calling as he prowled his way through the building. A sign saying staff cafeteria caught his eye. He headed in that direction.

"Oh, here you—" His cry of exuberance stopped dead. He gasped and took a step back. The men appeared lifeless. The first two he laid eyes on were slumped back in their chairs. The others lay on the floor, some with their upturned chairs beside them.

"Oh no. I don't believe this. Looks like ..." he shook his head. "Looks like they're all ... dead." He edged his way to the nearest team member and lifted the man's limp wrist, feeling for a pulse. "I'm sorry, Kat. There's no pulse. This fellow's stone cold. I'm wondering if what killed the emperors has killed your team. You'll have to get onto the authorities, Henri. This needs a thorough investigation. Hey, I can't take any more of this. I'm getting out of here."

Kyle bolted out the cafeteria door, panicking something evil might be lurking in the depths of the building. Once in the hallway, he scrambled past each open door keeping his eyes fixed on the exit. As he dashed from the building, he blew out a burst of relief. With one running jump onto the line, he commenced his ascent to the refuge of the hovering helicopter.

On his return to the Base, Kyle was met by a teary Kat and a poker-faced Henri. After giving Kat a consoling hug, he began recounting the gruesome scenes he'd just witnessed.

"I found it shocking enough stepping over the swathes of dead emperors, but finding your team had all perished was— " He stopped mid-sentence and bowed his head.

"After witnessing the scene at close hand, do you have any ideas on a likely cause?" Henri enquired.

He hung his head for a moment then gazed up. "I've been wracking my brain all the way back. A virus, maybe? Radiation? Or maybe some toxic gas penetrated up through the ice? Whatever it is, it's unparalleled. I have no knowledge of anything like this happening before. Never. Not anywhere."

"Don't worry," said Henri, "I've already contacted The Society in New York. Wonder what they'll make of it."

"The Society? You are joking aren't you? What's happened down here is unprecedented. This is history making stuff. We need to go straight to the top."

Henri wiped the sweat from his brow. "No. Just leave it to me, Kyle. The Society will deal with it."

"Nah. I don't agree. I'd be contacting some higher authorities. And the media. The world has a right to know. This may well be the start of some new and extremely dangerous virus. We don't want another one of those."

Henri took a long step back. "Well, if that's the case Kyle, you shouldn't be standing here talking to us. You need to be confined to quarantine." He turned to Kat for support.

"Can you see my point, Kat?"

She bit her lip and looked away.

"Not sure shutting me in quarantine's really necessary," said Kyle.

"But didn't you just tell Kat and me, the extinction might be caused by some unknown virus? I'm sorry, but we have to consider that possibility. I ask that you to remain in quarantine until we find out for sure what it was that killed the team. We'll leave your meals on a tray outside the door."

Kyle slapped his hand on his forehead. "Oh, this is ridiculous. Just crazy."

Henri raised his palm and took another step back. "No, not crazy. A preventive measure." Once again he looked to Kat. She stayed silent.

"We'll class it as precautionary prevention shall we? As your team leader, I'm ordering you to remain in your room until we determine the cause of the team's deaths."

After Kyle's reluctant departure for the Base clinic, Kat wiped away her tears and headed to the cafeteria. She wasn't surprised to hear Henri's fast paced footsteps hot on her heels. After pouring herself a coffee, she sat down at the table. A frown creased her face as he pulled out the chair next to hers.

"You okay, Kat?"

She sat silent for a moment wondering how she should confront him over his harsh treatment of Kyle.

"Tell me — Kyle — he's a member of your rescue team, right?" she put to him.

"Yes. Why?"

"It's just … I think you were very hard on him just now, especially after the brilliant job he's done—you know, rescuing me, and then braving it to check out the station. I can't begin to imagine the horrific scene the poor guy was forced to witness this morning."

Henri sat, unresponsive, stirring his coffee.

Kat crossed her legs, struggling not to kick him over his galling nonchalance.

"You know, Henri, Kyle's right about alerting the media. My team were struck down overnight. Imagine the havoc a global outbreak causing death this rapidly would wreak on the world."

She leaned forward over the table and gazed up, trying her hardest to eyeball him.

"You do realize, you'd be forever condemned by all humanity for delaying notification of something this devastating?"

He continued to sit, poker faced, oblivious to her point of view.

"Well, if you're not going to tell the authorities and the media, Henri, then I will."

Chapter Ten

Much to her disgust, Kat was unable to sway Henri into doing anything more than his rather pathetic protocol of contacting The World Ornithological Society in New York. She stormed out of the cafeteria, intent on airing her grievances to Ben.

The burly pilot froze as she rushed toward him. "What is it, Kat? You look even more upset now than you were earlier."

"Ooh …" she threw her hands in the air. "I've just been talking to Henri. I can't believe the stupidity of that man. He's in cloud cuckoo land. All he could come up with is contacting The Ornithological Society in New York. But you want to know the most ridiculous part?"

"What's that?"

"Did you know the man's not even an ornithologist? From what I remember his boss Levi telling me, he comes from a finance background."

"I'm just a pilot. Sorry, I can't offer you any ideas on who to contact. But yeah, what Kyle witnessed this morning is way more than scary. I'm with you all the way. Any suspicious deaths warrant top level investigation."

"Oh, and Ben," she whispered. "That little autopsy canister I handed you in the helicopter yesterday. You are forwarding it on to the UK address for me?"

"Yes, it'll be on the same plane out as the one to The Ornithological Society in New York."

"And you have kept your promise about keeping it just between you and me?"

"You have my word, Kat."

"Also, I want to ask you about those strange lights that lit up the sky last night."

"They were white flashing lights—high in the sky. All so bright. And in my line of work, I can tell you, flights humming around this area at night are extremely rare. I'm stumped as to what they were."

"It's just that Kyle mentioned radiation. But if it was some sort of nuke going off, we'd all be fried as well. Another thing he mentioned was the possibility of toxic gas coming up from under the ice. Do you think that might explain the strange lights you witnessed?"

"Hey, I'm no scientist. I don't know a thing about gases, or what activity might be brewing under Franklin Island."

He shrugged his broad shoulders. "Who knows, maybe the island's volcanic. So, there's another reason we need to get the experts in and have all these possibilities checked out."

"That's the next thing I wanted to ask you. Can I use the base's communications systems to let the world know what's going on down here?"

"Course you can. Our boss has gone back home—some sort of family crisis. But I can show you how our satellite system works. C'mon." He placed a comforting hand on her forearm. "I totally agree with you about the need to let the world know what's happened. And the sooner the better."

Kat spent the next hour locked in a desperate attempt to inform the outside world of the disaster that had annihilated the Antarctic team and the island's emperor penguins. But most of her time was spent wanting to hang up in frustration. Her ears prickled at a continuum of muffled voices and hushed background whisperings. The hesitant responses led to her realise her story was coming across as so outlandish, it was being taken for a hoax.

During her final attempt to notify a major world news service, she found herself raising her voice in anger. When asked if her boss could come to the phone, she wondered if she was being dismissed for nothing other than being a woman. She slammed down the receiver and ran for the solace of her room.

Fatigue and a sense of hopelessness left Kat so exhausted she fell into a late afternoon slumber. But her early evening doze was shattered by the thunderous roar of jet engines in reverse thrust. She raced from her room, eager to find out what aircraft had just touched down.

At the base's triple glazed entry doors, she spied Ben and Henri, and the other staff standing, waiting for the plane to taxi in. Henri's beaming grin told her he knew exactly what was happening. She looked away, keeping her eyes averted from his pompous face. Then with demure subtlety, she sidled up to Ben and motioned him to one side. "What's all this then, Ben?" she whispered in his ear.

"I've just been told this emergency flight was organised by the World Ornithological Society in New York. Henri says it's in response to his call. I'm told it's a small scientific team from Christchurch." Ben turned his eyes to the window and gestured. "I suppose they didn't have very far to travel—I'm sure the flying time is only four hours or so in that type of aircraft. Anyway, from what I've been told, this is just the start. We're about to have the place crawling with investigators, some coming from Australia as well."

"Just as well it's still autumn then. In a couple of weeks, we'll be blacked out in twenty-four-hour darkness and hampered by ice."

Kat shifted from one foot to the other as the grim faces of the first investigative team traipsed into the base. Henri rushed up to greet the leader, Kurt Matthews, a scruffily dressed man with an unruly grey beard. Kat eyed him up. *Has this guy just slept the night on a Christchurch park-bench or something?*

After trumpeting his high-ranking status in the World Ornithological Society, Henri turned and introduced each of the base team members one by one, leaving Kat until last. With a forced smile, she moved forward and shook each of their freezing cold hands.

Once the formal introductions were over, team leader, Kurt, moved in to address Henri.

"I'm afraid I have some very sad news for you, Henri. About your Society President, Levi Stanton. You'll be shocked to hear he passed away in Christchurch hospital early this morning."

After a cursory silence, Henri continued his laughing and joking with the team, patting them on the back and mouthing his appreciation for their commitment to investigating the mystery surrounding Franklin Island. Tears welled in Kat's eyes as she fought to make sense of the devastating news about the passing of her long-time friend. Hit with a sudden torrent of anguish, she reached out and grabbed Ben's arm for support.

Chapter Eleven

When Ben told Kat the base would soon be crawling with scientific investigators, he wasn't wrong. A second flight touched down just a few hours after the first. And that flight was followed by what turned out to be a most unsettling third.

Among the many new arrivals, Kat found herself drawn to the company of two fellow ornithologists, both intent on uncovering the reason for the bizarre behaviour of the emperor penguins and their subsequent demise. Although several years younger than herself, Juan, originally a Mexican native from Texas, and Athena from Canada, had been previously introduced to Kat by Levi, at a conference just two years prior. It soon became apparent Athena bore a curious admiration for Henri. Her already bubbly personality erupted to ecstasy the first time she spotted him on the base. "Hey, Henri, Henri!" She dashed up to welcome him, arms high in the air.

Kat cringed at their lengthy embrace.

Later, over lunch, Kat learned that Henri had lobbied for Society funding, allowing Athena to fly to Australia on a mission to study the habitat of the flamboyantly coloured but endangered Gouldian Finch.

"Oh," Athena gushed, "that man so deserves to take over the presidency from Levi Stanton. I just hope he wins the position. I'm pleased he appears so confident he will."

"But Henri's not an ornithologist. Wouldn't that make it difficult for him?" Kat asserted, straightening her posture in anticipation of a disapproving reply. But to her surprise, Athena agreed.

"Yes, I am worried that might be the case. You're not thinking of applying are you, Kat?"

"Oh …" Kat jumped with surprise. "Ah … to be honest, that's something I hadn't even considered. What about you guys?"

"No," Juan replied, "I've never been an employee of The Society, and I don't have enough experience—well, not yet. And I'm probably too young for such a high-ranking position."

Athena shifted uncomfortably in her chair. She didn't reply to Kat's question. Kat took it as an opportune moment to compliment Levi's lifetime devotion to his calling.

"It's going to be hard for anyone to fill Levi's shoes. Such an amazing man. I can't believe he's gone."

That night after she'd retired to her room, Kat lay on her bed, ruminating about Henri and his presumption he'd win Levi Stanton's President position. The longer she mulled it over, the more convinced she became of the man's unsuitability.

"Yes," she murmured to herself, raising her head in the darkened room. "Why not. I have all the experience to perform Levi's role way better than Henri ever could. Anyway, what have I got to lose by applying?" She flopped back down, and in contented repose, fell asleep.

Next morning, Kat was awoken by a loud and persistent rap, rap, rap on her door. She heaved a harried sigh. "Okay, okay, I won't be a minute," she called out as she struggled into her clothes.

The hinges squeaked as she prised the door open to a rather guarded crack.

"Oh … it's you, Ben … so early. What is it?" she cried.

"I'm in shock, Kat." He puffed out his distress. "It's Kyle. Looks as though he's taken too many sleeping pills. One of the investigations team spied his uneaten dinner tray outside his door. Fortunately, this guy happens to be a medic. He's in with him now."

"Oh no," Kat wailed. "He was probably traumatised by the scene at the station—seeing all those dead bodies. And then that damn Henri locking him up in quarantine straight after. Sorry, Ben, but I'm so angry at that man for the way he mistreated poor Kyle."

"I know, I know."

Kat opened her arms for a long and comforting hug.

"Any news this morning on how the investigations are going?" Kat mumbled into the warmth of Ben's chest.

"I was on my way to the morning briefing in the cafeteria when I was told about Kyle."

Kat let go her clench. "I'm wondering if the results of their emperor brain inspection will be announced today?"

"The briefing was scheduled for 8 a.m. How about we go and have breakfast? That way we can stay and listen in—find out what's happening."

The cafeteria had filled to a crowd. After breakfast, the leaders of both teams stood in turn and presented their findings from their first day of investigations on Franklin

Island. The preliminary examination of the bodies of the station team revealed visible evidence of swelling of the brain. There also appeared to be some evidence of an inexplicable puncture mark to the skin covering the neurocranium. But the leader qualified his statement by stipulating that a more thorough autopsy would need to be facilitated to determine the cause of death.

Investigations into the mass demise of the emperor penguins by the second team revealed the same brain enlargement. Their leader also confirmed the brain swelling had previously been observed by 'a Franklin Island ornithologist'. They also divulged that world media were anxious for news on the deaths, and the situation had sparked unsettling global speculation and unparallelled panic.

"All sounding kind of weird, eh?" said Ben, as he and Kat sat watching the teams exit the cafeteria for their second day of investigations.

"I don't know what to think. And they obviously still don't know what caused the swelling in the emperor's brains. But right now, I'm more worried about Kyle. Who'd ever have guessed such a happy, easy-going guy would have needed sleeping medication?"

"Yeah, but don't forget, any career in saving people from danger is going to put the rescuer at risk of being exposed to some horrific situations."

As they spoke, their ears pricked up at the sound of another plane landing outside the base.

"That's odd," said Ben. "I was told there were no more planes coming in. Our accommodations pretty well filled to capacity."

Kat rose to her feet. "Let's go to the entrance and find out who it is. My guess is it's a news team. The media will have been itching to be here at ground zero."

When they reached the twin potted palms gracing the entry doors, Kat was surprised to find there was no one there to greet whoever might be on the flight.

She turned to Ben. "How odd? Henri's usually here to meet everyone arriving at the base."

Ben surveyed the area. "Well, he was here, just a second ago. I saw him take a quick scan, then disappear again."

He shook his head. "That guy is seriously strange."

As they stood facing the tarmac, they spotted two women wearing some sort of uniform approaching the doors.

"They look more like police officers," said Ben. "C'mon, seeing as Henri's not here, we'll say hello and find out who they are."

After the uniformed pair entered the building, Ben strode up to greet them and introduced himself.

"Hi," the first woman, who was obviously in charge replied. "I'm Officer Teresa Carter. We're Australian police officers, we're here to interview a Ms. Katrina Ingledew."

"Oh … that's me. I'm Katrina Ingledew," said Kat, her eyes widening as she stepped forward.

"Is there somewhere private we can talk, Ms. Ingledew?" the officer enquired.

"Aah …" she looked to Ben. "What about the communications room? Would that be okay for us to go in there, Ben?"

"Aah … yeah. That's okay." He was left in gawking bewilderment as Kat escorted them away.

A panicky trembling racked Kat's legs as she closed the communications room door and invited the officers to sit down.

"Our time at this base is very limited, so I'll get straight to the point, Ms. Ingledew. We're here to interview you over an allegation you deliberately abandoned your Franklin Island team when their lives were in danger. It's been alleged, your negligence in supervisory due care resulted in their deaths."

Kat closed her eyes and slumped forward in her chair. All she pictured was Henri's smirking face.

Chapter Twelve

Kat opened her eyes and straightened in her chair. She steepled her hands under her chin pausing in a momentary whirl of contemplation.

"And do you know the real reason I was forced to leave the team at the station?" she questioned the police officer. "Because what you've just told me is exaggerated fiction. Nothing more than a made-up story."

"That's precisely why we're here, Ms. Ingledew," replied Officer Carter. Her hazel eyes pierced Kat's. "We're here to document your reasons for abandoning your team."

"Well … your enquiries are based on incorrect information. I want to know who made this allegation against me."

"We're unable to disclose that information."

Kat raised her voice. "Oh … so now I'm getting the infamous 'no comment' from you lot am I?"

The two officers averted their eyes.

"The reason I was forced to leave Franklin Island was because the food supply had run out. I attempted to evacuate the whole team, but the others refused to go. They'd already begun consuming penguin meat." She crinkled her nose in disgust. "As you probably know, my profession's an ornithologist. I refuse to eat the species I study. I'd have starved to death if I hadn't got myself out of there."

Kat sank back in her chair convinced she'd credibly justified her reason for not being able to remain at the station.

Officer Carter paused her scribbling. "And is anyone able to confirm what you're telling us? That is, provide evidence to back up your claim the Franklin Station's food supply ran out?"

Kat turned her eyes to the ceiling. "No, I don't have a witness," she snapped. "It's pretty damn obvious there's no-one but me left alive in the team—isn't that the reason you're here?" She crossed her arms tightly across her body.

An electrifying silence stilled the air.

Officer Carter looked up from her note taking. "Now, I have to inform you, Ms. Ingledew, there's also a second charge we're required to question you about."

Kat scowled at the officer.

"Yes, the Manager of your Antarctic program received a complaint from one of your staff members; a Mr. Dario Cross, on the day prior to you abandoning your team. The gentleman, Mr Cross, lodged an on-line allegation you physically assaulted him. He also claimed you violated your code of discipline in martial arts. He uploaded images of the severe bruising your alleged assault caused him. Mr Cross also claimed he was left with an inability to walk."

"Pfft …" Kat blew out her disgust. "I have a witness here on the base who can justify my act of self defence against Dario Cross. The man became angry because I refused to eat penguin meat—whinged about me consuming all the team's food supplies. He grabbed me by the throat. I was convinced he was going to strangle me. This was no assault on my part. I was provoked into fighting him off. I fought to save my life. My actions were purely self-defence."

"Okay then, and who is this witness?"

"Our helicopter pilot, Kyle. I informed him of the attack as soon as he transported me to the safety of the base."

"We'll obtain a statement from him then."

"I doubt you'll be able to interview Kyle today. He took too many sleeping meds last night. You're probably going to have to wait until he recovers."

The moment she exited the communications room, Kat scanned the area for Ben. Her heart missed a beat when he was nowhere to be found. But as she turned the corner, she spied him pacing the corridor. He spun around at the cry of his name and raced toward her.

"What in hell was that all about?" he demanded to know.

His mouth gaped open as Kat detailed the allegations made against her.

"I don't believe this," she moaned. "It's as though someone is out to blacken my good name."

"So, what's going to happen?"

"The officers are going to talk to Kyle to confirm what I said to him when I was rescued. Remember? I did tell you later that day how Dario grabbed me by the throat and tried to strangle me. Ooh," she shuddered, "I just hope he's recovered enough to remember what I told him that day."

Ben invited Kat to the sanctuary of his room following her ordeal with the two police officers.

"Wow!" she exclaimed as he opened the door. "This is a luxury hotel suite compared to my shoebox. Oh yes, I'd forgotten. You did say you had a window." Her brow raised as she surveyed the generous size of the room. "This is nothing like my dingy little rathole."

Ben grinned. "Yeah, this is what you get when you fly birds instead of studying them."

He closed the door and motioned her to one of the seats beside a round glass-topped coffee table. Then he began rubbing his tummy. "Like some chocolate, Kat?" he asked as he opened the fridge.

"No thanks, but you go ahead."

They both relaxed back on the lounge and before long began divulging details of the lives they led away from the daily grind of the Antarctic. Kat was surprised to learn Ben was the father of two young daughters. He disclosed how his relationship had ended when their mother succumbed to the downward spiral of an ongoing drug addiction. He expressed his gratitude to his mother for taking over their care.

"I miss my kids more than words can say, but at least I don't worry about them. My mom's the best parent any child could ever wish for."

They sat for a moment in reflective silence.

"And what about you, Kat? Who figures in your life back in Australia?"

She cringed. *Why does this question come up every time I befriend a man?*

"I own a small terrace house in Sydney. Can't really call it home 'cos I'm hardly ever there. And when I am there, I like to keep fit—you know, gym and martial arts." She paused with discomfort, knowing she was avoiding the real question.

"And …?"

She squirmed. "Well … no. There's no one—as you say, who figures in my life. I'm afraid I'll never commit myself to a man again."

"Once bitten, eh?"

She looked away. "I was once… Oh, I might as well tell you the whole story. I was once engaged … yes, to a guy who lived in my neighbourhood. And I was stupid enough to think we had the most perfect relationship. So much so, we even shared keys to each other's houses."

Ben grinned.

"Yes, Ben, it was *that* good. Or so I assumed. Anyway, I woke early one morning and thought to myself, I'll treat him to a surprise cooked breakfast. I packed up some eggs and bacon and walked around to find he had someone else in his bed."

Ben scrunched up his face.

"I stifled my pain by devoting myself to my job. And because he lived nearby, I deliberately stayed away from home as much as my career allowed." She heaved a sigh and stroked her cheek. "Anyway, I'm probably too old now to have the children I always dreamed of."

Ben picked up on the heartache in her voice. He switched to a different subject.

"Tell me, Kat. What's your take on our tragedy down here—you know, the deaths of all your team?"

Kat told Ben how she'd tossed and turned the last two nights, pondering on that very mystery. She revealed she couldn't help but feel their deaths were something to do with their consumption of penguin meat. She said she'd observed rapid changes in their temperament. How they became locked in a world of their own. Unable to reason. Almost as though their thinking—their cognitive processing had deserted them.

"Your penguin meat theory is interesting. "It might explain why they wouldn't leave the station when their food ran out, especially when winter was closing in."

Kat eyed her watch. "I wonder how the police are going with questioning Kyle. You know, Ben, I can't help but suspect it was Henri who orchestrated this vendetta against me. Hah, like you said, peering around the corner as the police were arriving in the base, then disappearing. Says it all, doesn't it?"

"But why would he want to do that to you, Kat?"

"I may be wrong, but you know the graduate ornithologist, Athena? She asked me whether I'm going to apply for Levi Stanton's position. Don't you think it strange she'd even ask me that? I mean … that presumption hadn't even entered my head."

Ben professed his suspicion with an extended *hmmm.*

"But after mulling it over, I reckon I'd be every bit as suitable for the role as Henri. The guy's not even an ornithologist." She paused for a moment, deep in thought. "Trouble is, I doubt I'd even get a look in. Both times I visited Levi at The Society, I noticed their management staff were ninety nine percent male. It's as though they're stuck in a time warp."

Ben flashed her a toothy grin. "So will *you* be the one to jolt them into the 21st century then, Kat?"

Chapter Thirteen

Following her outpouring of painful revelations over her fiancée's cruel betrayal, Kat emerged from Ben's room, eager to find out how the police had progressed with their interview with Kyle.

She tracked the officers down in the seating area of the panoramic glassed entrance to the base. It came as no surprise to Kat to find them huddled together in deep conversation with Henri. Kat stiffened. She crept towards them, her ears pricked for any mention of her name, or whisperings about the fabricated allegations she'd been slapped with.

Henri turned his head when the two officers suddenly peered right past him. He froze at Kat's scowling presence.

"Ah, I guessed it must have been you, Henri. It was you who made the allegation about me abandoning my responsibility to my team, wasn't it?" Henri's face flushed crimson. Without so much as a murmur, he stood to his feet and skulked off.

Kat swore under her breath as he made his exit. After he'd slunk away, she sat down to address Officer Carter.

"I've been trying to find you. I'm assuming Kyle backed me up on why I was forced to leave Franklin Island?"

"No, he didn't. Your witness appeared quite disorientated when we interviewed him. To be honest, he presented in a state of confusion. Even his speech was slurred. We weren't able to get anything meaningful out of him."

Kat jumped to her feet. Her hands flew straight to her hips. "Well, I'm telling you now, this accusation I abandoned my team is a lie. I want my good name cleared right now."

"Can't see that happening anytime soon," Officer Carter asserted. "And don't forget you also have an outstanding charge of assault on Mr Dario Cross. I should tell you that despite Mr Cross being deceased, it's very likely you'll be receiving a summons to appear in an Australian court."

"What? Oh, that's absurd."

Kat spent the rest of the day in the consoling company of Ben. How she valued his moral support. Despite the accusations she'd been slapped with haunting her every waking moment, with Ben at her side she felt safe. Reassured. But best of all, there were no tiresome overtones of masculine neediness. On so many occasions in the past, the lecherous expectations of men had ruined a burgeoning friendship. The warm cocoon of both his genial company and his plush room had her relaxing back, savouring a sense of contentment she hadn't experienced in a long, long time.

An early morning knock on her door reminded Kat of Ben's promise to wake her the next day. He'd figured how anxious she'd be to hear the results of day two of the investigations into the deaths of the Franklin Island team.

The mouth-watering aroma of sizzling bacon spiced the air as Kat and Ben entered the already bustling cafeteria for breakfast. While waiting in the self-help buffet queue, Kat searched the seating area in the hope she'd spot Kyle. But once again, he wasn't there. Her head drooped as the same dark image of him locked up in quarantine flashed through her mind. Just another reason to despise Henri for all the misery he'd inflicted on poor Kyle.

After filling his plate with piled-high servings of bacon and eggs, Ben found a setting for two and sat waiting for Kat. As she placed her plate on the table, he gawked at what he considered to be meagre pickings.

She registered the incredulous stare on his face. "I know, I know," she said, eyeing his bumper serving. "You're going to tell me I need more food than this to survive my day."

He let out a chuckle. "I know better than to nag a woman about what she should and shouldn't eat."

His eyes skimmed her taut body. It would not have been the first time Ben had discerned the total absence of fat on Kat's athletic figure.

As had happened on the previous morning after breakfast, the first leader of the two investigative teams made his way to the front of the cafeteria to present an update on yesterday's developments. The room fell deathly silent when the leader officially confirmed their findings of mysterious puncture-like incisions to the neurocraniums of each of the Franklin Island victims. But a clamour of gasps buzzed out when he revealed his scientific team also found evidence fluid had been extracted from each of their swollen brains. There was even more commotion when the second team leader stepped up to announce proof of a similar extraction of excess brain fluid on a deceased emperor body found at the station door.

"This is getting more and more creepy," Kat whispered to Ben. "To think, I'd have been a victim too if you hadn't come to my rescue."

"Yes, and I have to wonder what those guys in your team must have endured—what horror they must have witnessed before they died."

Kat's eyes widened in dark contemplation.

"You know, Kat? I keep wondering about those strange lights outside my window that night.

Kat let out an exaggerated shudder. "I don't even want to think about that."

Chapter Fourteen

Officer Carter's warning she'd be facing a court appearance on her return to Australia unsettled Kat. Her stomach grumbled and churned all morning. All she wanted was to get into the base clinic and prompt Kyle on his recall of the epic day he lowered himself down the helicopter line to rescue her.

As the morning wore on, the desire to question Kyle consumed Kat.

"I can't stand not knowing what's going to happen to me," she moaned to Ben.

"I can see that. You're so darned fidgety. I'll try having a word in Luke's ear. Luke's our base nurse. I'll ask if he'd be willing to let you in to talk to Kyle."

"Oh, would you? Please, Ben." Kat's face morphed from tense to excited. "Apart from sounding him out about his memory, I'd like to know how he's doing after his overdose."

"Okay, leave it with me."

Kat cocooned herself into Ben's luxuriously soft sofa, calmer in the knowledge his idea might help prove her innocence over the outlandish police allegations.

Ben wasn't gone long. He stumbled back in the door, poker faced.

"What is it, Ben? You look so serious."

"Sorry, Kat. I didn't manage to persuade Luke to allow Kyle a visitor. I have to say, he was strangely uneasy about the idea. Wouldn't look me in the eye. It's almost as if a bar has been placed on Kyle talking to anyone."

"Hah, that'd be right. It's that bastard, Henri. Got me cornered in every way."

"I still can't quite fathom what this is all about with you and Henri."

"But I did tell you, Ben," she said, raising her voice. "He sees me as a threat to his career path. Why else would Athena have queried my professional intentions? I've pondered long and hard about what she said. There wouldn't have been any other reason Henri would have discussed his career prospects with her. And don't forget he personally authorised funding Athena for a major ornithological project. He already had her on side."

"Yeah … I suppose. As you say, what other reason would he have to accuse you of deliberately abandoning your team?"

"Hmm, come to think of it, there may be another reason. My guess is, Henri despises the fact it was me leading the team when news of the emperor mystery broke. *Noted ornithologist, Katrina Ingledew,* was the headline, and he didn't like the credit attached to my name."

"Oh yeah, hadn't thought of that."

"Listen, Ben, surely Luke doesn't stay with Kyle twenty-four hours a day? He must go to lunch. How about you sneak me in to talk to him while he's in the cafeteria? I'll only need a minute."

"Course he goes to lunch." Ben eyed his watch and rubbed his tummy.

Kat grinned. "Oh, it's that word *lunch*, isn't it? Thinking of your belly again, eh? Why don't you go now—

have yourself an early bite to eat and wait for Luke to appear?"

The plan was laid. Ben would dine early and stay until Luke arrived. Then as soon as Luke sat down, he'd slip out and escort Kat into the clinic.

Ben was halfway through his second chocolate pudding when he spotted Luke joining the buffet queue. He gulped down the creamy remains on his plate and made a discreet exit.

Kat gasped when the door to her room flew open. "Now, Kat. Now. Quick! Luke's in there now selecting his lunch."

She jumped to her feet and raced after Ben.

"Yes," he puffed peering through the crack of the opening clinic door. "All clear. In you go. I'll stay out here—stand guard for you. But if I knock, be ready to run." He opened the door and Kat bolted in. Her nostrils smarted at the overpowering reek of bleach.

"Kat…? Is that… Oh, it is you. Thanks for coming," Kyle rasped as he sat up. "I've been wondering when I'd get to see you again."

"How are you, Kyle? I've been so worried."

His skin ghosted deathly pale, making his face appear gaunt.

"I'm okay. Don't know whether you heard, but I did a stupid thing. It's a long story." He pointed to a locked cupboard. "They have me on antidepressants. But I swear, they're making me feel worse. Not getting any better at all. Luke chucked an empty pill sachet in that bin there early this morning. Can you get someone to check them out for me?"

"It's not right, you being held here. Anyway, let me find out what meds they've got you on."

Kat rummaged through the bin for the spent packaging and found the name on the back of the wrapper.

"Hmm, Petrazine. No. Sorry, I don't know this one." The empty wrapper crackled as she scrunched it up in her hand.

"Tell me Kyle. Have the police been asking you about me and my team? You know—whether or not they refused to leave Franklin Island?"

A frown of confusion furrowed his brow. He shot her a blank look and said he couldn't remember.

Officer Carter was right. Kyle wasn't even capable of remembering the police interviewing him, let alone the events of the day of her rescue.

The danger of getting sprung in the clinic suddenly spooked Kat. She squeezed Kyle's frozen hand in hers and wished him well.

"Phew." Ben's eyes lit up. "Am I pleased to see you? I've been panicking someone might come around the corner any minute."

"C'mon, Ben. Let's get outta here. I've got something to show you."

Once they reached the refuge of his room, Kat unwrinkled the medication sachet she'd concealed in her hand.

"Here. Take a look at this. Kyle says they have him on an antidepressant called Petrazine. I have no knowledge of such a drug. He reckons it's making him feel worse."

Ben studied the label. "Hey, I know this drug. I had a cousin who was once on Petrazine. It's not an antidepressant. It's an antipsychotic. Why would they have him on antipsychotic medication for depression? I reckon a drug of this class would add to his confusion."

"That'd be right. Someone doesn't want him telling the truth, do they? Mark my words Ben, Henri's behind this. I'm going straight to the police. C'mon, we'll inform officer Carter."

A biting fear the two police officers might have already returned to Australia gnawed at Kat as she raced around the base on a determined mission to locate them.

Chapter Fifteen

The response Kat received from Officer Carter about the inappropriateness of Kyle's medication was less than enthusiastic. She served Kat a sharp reminder she'd trained as a police officer, and Kat, as an ornithologist, adding neither had the qualifications of a doctor.

Kat's penetrating gaze into Officer Carter's hazel eyes conveyed her craving for recognition for her very own detective work.

"But Ben here has firsthand knowledge of the drug Petrazine. He had a family member who was prescribed it for psychosis. The drug's an antipsychotic for goodness sakes, it's not an antidepressant. Ben says it's no wonder Kyle has no memory of the day I was rescued."

"I just told you, I don't have authority to give staff advice on medical matters. I suggest you find a medical doctor or talk to whoever's administering the drug."

Ben placed his arm around Kat's waist. "That would be Luke, our base nurse. C'mon, time we confronted him head on."

Kat huffed. "He'll only deny it. No one around here tells the truth about anything."

After Ben and Kat left Officer Carter, he suggested they wait until the day's limited internet link became available and research the drug themselves. "At least we'll gain an accurate answer on its prescribed usage."

"Just as well I booked us some computer time," said Ben logging on to the base internet. There were three other base members already lined up waiting for access.

"Might have a quick look at the world news first," he whispered. "Find out what they're all saying about our situation down here."

Kat stood alongside while he scanned the screen. As he scrolled down, a news headline about the Antarctic deaths caught his eye. "They're still talking about some sort of contaminant or virus. Hmm … there's also a theory it may have been spread by oral ingestion of penguin meat."

He kept scrolling then let out a sudden gasp. "Oh Kat. You're not going to like what I'm seeing here."

"What is it?" She shuffled in close and leaned forward in an attempt to peruse the adjacent news item.

Ben pointed to the headline. "Somehow the media have found out about the accusation you abandoned your team."

"What? But it's only an allegation. How dare they say anything, especially when it hasn't been proved."

"Appears you're another victim of trial by media. Obviously someone's leaked that information."

"Yeah, I damn well know who that would be. Ooh, I've had a gutful of that man. I'm going to confront him head on."

"Listen, before you jump in headfirst, it might pay to check whether it was the police who made the media aware of the charge. But can I ask you to hold fire for a minute? I want to go to a therapeutic drugs site and get the low down on Petrazine. Sorry, Kat, but there's other staff waiting to get internet access."

Kat stamped from one foot to another as Ben typed in a keyboard clattering search for a list of treatment applications for the drug Kyle had been prescribed. It wasn't long before he raised an applauding fist in the air. Ben's memory had been spot-on. Petrazine was definitely not recommended for use as an antidepressant.

Armed with information about the inappropriateness of Petrazine for Kyle's depression, coupled with proof of a leak to the media of the charge against her, Kat was busting for a showdown with Officer Carter.

"Yes, I'm well aware of that leak to the media, Ms. Ingledew," Officer Carter replied to Kat's complaint. "I'm always up to date with all news reports. And although your position as team leader is indeed referred to, there's no mention of your name. So … in that case, I doubt any action can be taken against the media, or against the person who provided the information."

"But who was it? Who would do a thing like that?"

Officer Carter shrugged her shoulders. "Perhaps it was the Manager of your Antarctic programme. I don't know. You tell me."

"I'm certain it was Henri Dubois. That man's out to blacken my good name. He sees me as his rival for the top position in The World Ornithological Society."

Officer Carter didn't answer. She looked away.

"And I must tell you, Ben checked out a therapeutic drug site. The medication the clinic has Kyle on is definitely not for depression. So, he's not on the correct medication. Petrazine is an anti-psychotic drug. Ben says the therapeutic drug site clearly states the drug causes confusion. That would explain why he can't answer your questions about the day of my rescue."

Once again Officer Carter sat silent.

Kat raised her voice. "Are you even listening to what I'm saying?"

"I did hear you Ms Ingledew! We will investigate. Now please. Leave."

The gloominess enveloping Kat over the response she received from Officer Carter matched the pitch-black day outside. The Antarctic seasonal norm of twenty-four-hour darkness had finally descended. Now Ben had become her rock, all she wanted was to run to him and vent her feelings of injustice.

There was no answer when Kat knocked on Ben's door. She'd come to know him so well. His passion for food would have beckoned him to an early lunch.

She was right. His familiar beefy form was sitting, head hunched forward over his overfilled plate.

"Oh, Ben," she exclaimed as she sat down. "Don't tell me you're eating again."

"Why not? better than starving myself to anorexia like you're doing."

Kat stiffened at his remark.

"Oh … sorry Kat," he reached out his hand. "I didn't mean that like it sounded."

"But how can I eat? I'm so wound up over what's going on. It's like the whole world's against me."

"No, your name wasn't even mentioned in the news. Believe me, the whole world doesn't know."

"Yes, but everyone at The Ornithological Society will know. I don't stand a chance of landing a job there now."

"By the way, Kat. Maybe I've forgotten, but remember the day Kyle rescued you? You did tell him one of your team assaulted you, and that was the reason you had to use your martial arts expertise?"

"Yes, I distinctly remember telling him, Dario had grabbed me by the throat. I thought I'd told you that before, Ben. Why do you ask?"

"It's just that when his memory does return, he'll be able to prove your innocence."

Kat rolled her eyes. "I'd already worked that out, Ben."

Ben let out a gasp. "Hey, Kat, do you realize with everything that's been going on today, we both missed the morning briefing on the investigation."

"Oh! Oh no … so, we did."

"Don't worry, I just had a message from one of my team. You won't believe the latest. They've discovered strange shoe prints in the room where your team were found dead."

"Shoeprints?"

"Yeah, shoeprints. And they're not Franklin Station issue footwear. They don't belong to any of the team. Now how creepy is that?"

Chapter Sixteen

"I've had enough of this bullshit," Kat ranted. "What do you reckon Ben? I'm so ready to confront Luke right now—find out who authorised the wrong treatment for Kyle. You willing to join me?"

Ben cleared his throat. "Don't know that's our role, Kat—to confront Luke. Shouldn't the police be doing that?"

"Hah, might as well go to my room and pack my bags for Sydney. I'll be waiting forever if I wait for Officer Carter to do anything. Damn," she cried, burying her face in her hands, "I give up!"

She turned to go.

"Okay, okay," he said, reaching out his hand. "I get your point."

"Well come on then, let's get it over and done with. Right now. While I'm in the mood."

Ben exhaled a compliant sigh then followed behind Kat as she stormed off in the direction of the clinic.

Her thumping rap on the clinic door matched Kat's bristling anger. When Luke opened up, she barged in.

"What's up, guys?" he asked, taking a step backwards.

"Where's Kyle?" she enquired.

"Aah … taking a shower … I think." He sniffed the air. "Yuk! Yes, I can almost taste the shampoo."

"I want to talk to you about his condition. He told me the meds he's on aren't helping his depression. Ben checked out the medication he's been prescribed. That drug's no antidepressant, Luke. We want to know what's going on."

His face bore a hint of amusement. "Hmm, and where did you two get your mental health qualifications? As well as gaining my Bachelor of Nursing, I'm a fully qualified psychiatric nurse practitioner. Believe me, I have prescribed Luke the correct medication. The man has what's termed depressive psychosis. He suffers hallucinations, delusions, and confusion. I had no qualms whatsoever about prescribing Petrazine for his condition."

Kat froze. An awkward silence hung in the air. "Okay …" she mumbled, her voice flat with resignation.

She scrambled out of the clinic with Ben hot on her heels.

"I feel such a fool," said Kat. "I really thought Kyle was being kept in a deliberate state of confusion."

"I must say, you had me convinced too."

"What am I going to do now, Ben? The Australian courts aren't going to believe what I was forced to endure on Franklin Island. Not unless I have Kyle as my witness. I'm going to lose my career. It's like … my whole world's falling apart."

Ben sat for a moment in deep contemplation. "How about I come to Sydney with you? You've confided enough in me. I can act as your witness for the charges you're facing."

Although thankful for Ben's unwavering support, a sudden sense of being smothered riled Kat. *Why is it, whenever I allow myself to get close to a man, I end up feeling stifled? As though he wants to take over. As though he's trying to control me at a time I'm feeling most vulnerable.*

Kat studied Ben. Suddenly, those big fun-filled eyes didn't exude so much delight. She looked away.

"That's kind of you, Ben, but no. You can't just up and leave your job."

"Why not? There's not a lot I can—" His words were interrupted by a gentle knock on the door.

"Hello," said a grey bearded man as the door opened. "I'm Kurt Matthews. Don't know whether you remember me. I'm leading the Franklin Island investigative team. I was told Katrina Ingledew might be with you."

"Yes, she is in here." Ben opened the door wide. "She's sitting right here on my sofa."

Kurt peered into the room. "Ah, Katrina, how are you? Do you remember me? Kurt Matthews. We met on my arrival from Christchurch."

Kat hesitated. "Ah … yes I do." She recalled her first impression of Kurt, the day he walked into the base. To her, he looked like some old vagrant who'd just slept the night on a Christchurch park-bench.

Kurt began with idle chatter, stroking his scruffy grey beard as he spoke. Then came a bolt from the blue.

"Listen Kat. We're organizing a research team to undertake some field work in Tierra del Fuego. It appears the situation there's just one step behind what happened to the penguin population on Franklin Island. I know they're a different species of penguin, but they're exhibiting the same symptoms you first described with your emperors. Had you heard anything about this?"

"No. I had no idea."

"I'm aware you're the only ornithologist with first-hand experience of the Franklin Island disaster, so I was hoping you'd be willing to lend your expertise to the team we're setting up for Chile."

Kat looked at Ben, her mouth gaping. Fleeting thoughts flashed through her brain.

At last, I can get myself out of this hole I'm in. And I can advance my career.

"I … oh yes, Kurt, I'd be up for that challenge. Yes. Sounds great."

"Good, good. But we must fly out ASAP—while we're still getting a reasonable glimmer of daylight on the horizon and the cold isn't too extreme.

"No worries. I can be packed and ready, whenever you want to leave. But please, Kurt, please don't tell anyone I'm coming with you."

Chapter Seventeen

A brief and unsettling silence followed Kurt Matthew's departure from Ben's room. A wide beam cheered Kat's face. *Why isn't Ben congratulating me on the invitation to join the investigative team in Tierra del Fuego?*

"Hey, what do you think of that, Ben?" she cried, her eyes sparkling with excitement.

"I can't believe it. Just when everything had turned so hopeless for me. Then out of the blue comes an offer like this."

Ben kept his gaze fixed to the floor. Head slightly bowed. Silent.

"Ben? Are you okay?"

He lifted his head and looked away.

"What is it, Ben? I expected you'd be happy for me getting out of the hole I'm in here."

"But I was really looking forward to going to Sydney with you. You know; supporting you through your court ordeal."

"Oh …"

"Kat?" He moved in close and looked into her eyes. "Would you … ?" He looked away then returned his gaze. "Would you … marry me?"

She squirmed and drew back in her seat.

"Marry …?"

"Yes, come home with me to White Plains and meet my two daughters—my family."

Her face creased with a quizzical expression. "But, Ben. We hardly know each other. Why would you want us to get married?"

"Kat, you're the only woman I've ever known who's like a friend to me."

"But your wife. Wasn't she … a friend?"

Ben started waffling, telling her about his ex-wife's constant emotional fragility. His voice tremored as he painted a heartrending tale about his marriage being a one way take fest: a take he described as a long and draining dependency. The kind of take that offered nothing back. Kat registered the quivering desperation in his voice. He was about to break.

She fought for her breath as she struggled to her feet. The very idea of committing to a man again was too much.

"I'm sorry, Ben," she said after withdrawing to the blackness of the window. "You're a really nice guy and I enjoy your company, but a relationship is … well, to be honest, the very thought of a commitment to any man still scares the hell out of me."

"It's just … what you said about wanting to have children, I can't get that out of my mind."

"That is my one regret in life. But I've resigned myself to knowing I'm past that now."

"Well, my two daughters need a mother. You're the only woman I've ever met I'd feel comfortable about fulfilling that role."

"That's very sweet, Ben. And I do take that as a compliment. But didn't you tell me your mother was the best at raising them?"

"She is. But Mom's getting older. She needs time for herself; for all her hobbies and her friends."

Although she sat back down, Kat perched uneasily on the arm of the sofa. Ben reached out for her hand.

"Don't, Ben. Please don't," she said folding her arms across her chest. "I told you how my dreams were shattered all those years ago. The wounds haven't healed. I honestly don't know if I'll ever be ready to trust again."

Ben withdrew his hand and let it fall to the sofa. He slumped forward and once again lowered his gaze to the floor.

Kat sensed more than just disappointment. She was witnessing a side of Ben she hadn't seen before. He was acting as though he refused to believe he was being rejected. Like a little boy. A rather spoilt little boy. A boy accustomed to getting everything he wants in life.

I wonder if that's how he ended up getting his mother to take responsibility for his children. And what about his marriage? What wife would put up with a man who won't take 'no' from a woman?

Kat battled to shrug off any sense of guilt by deliberately changing the subject to her forthcoming assignment in Tierra del Fuego. Although she attempted to get Ben to talk, encouraging him to air his views on what might be going on in South America, he maintained a sullen disposition, keeping his eyes averted.

A second visit to Ben's room by Kurt Matthews, rescued Kat from the uncomfortable undercurrent that had blunted the air following her brush-off of his marriage proposal. Her face lit up the minute Kurt's voice called out at the door.

"Hi, Kat," he said peering in. "Just calling to let you know the Punta Arenas team will be flying out after our morning update in the cafeteria tomorrow. You'll be ready?"

"I'll be ready. Got to go and pack," she cried, her stare focussed on the door. "See you at tomorrow morning's briefing."

Relieved to return to the respite of her own room, Kat threw herself down on the bed and huffed an exasperated sigh.

"Why?" she muttered, staring up at the ceiling. "Why did *he* have to go and put that on me when we've only known each other a short time?"

After sorting her meagre ration of base clothes and personal items into a small carry bag, she crawled in under the bed covers and fell into a long and peaceful sleep.

Finding Ben sitting alone and forlorn in the cafeteria next morning, sparked a fleeting moment of guilt in Kat. He had, after all, proved a constant companion. He'd also supported her through the cruel mudslinging thrown at her by Henri and Officer Carter.

Once she'd selected her breakfast, she pulled up a chair next to Ben and sat down.

"And how are you this morning, Ben?" she murmured in a warm comforting voice.

"Yeah, okay. I'm okay. I had a think about what I said yesterday, and I realize now how stupid I was. Let's just leave it there."

Kat nodded her approval. "I'm looking forward to this morning's briefing. Hopefully there'll be an update about what's going on in Tierra del Fuego."

After they'd munched over an unusually subdued breakfast, Ben and Kat sat back to listen in on the morning briefing. As usual, the leader of each of the two teams stood to present their findings from the previous day's investigations.

Although Kat muttered her disappointment at not hearing any first-up news on Tierra del Fuego, the revelations from the Franklin Island squad cast a shadowy atmosphere over the proceedings. It appeared the members investigating the deaths of the team had been so preoccupied studying the neurocranial incisions, they had missed spotting an unexplained punch mark on the left hand of each of the team's bodies.

"Each team member has something resembling a punch biopsy on the top of their left hand," the leader of the team announced. "Now we need to determine whether there may have been a time lag between the punch biopsies and the neurocranium incisions."

Next on the list of revelations came more information on the mysterious footprints found near the dead bodies.

"We engaged the world's leading footwear specialists to study these prints. Yet not one expert can come up with a manufactured product matching those tread impressions."

Chapter Eighteen

A faint luminous glow bathed the far horizon as Kat concealed herself in the midst of the team huddling at the entrance to the base. Her heart raced as she waited to board the aircraft transporting them to Punta Arenas in Chile. *Will I make my escape without being spotted by Officer Carter?*

As the group moved to the exit door, the early morning's cloud free aura bathed the tarmac. The light was an eerie pastel—a daylight barely brighter than a decent moonlight.

The moment the huge glass doors parted, Kat began shivering as the frigid air stung her face. The reek of aviation fuel prickled her nose. She hung back at the rear of the group, her head spinning in anticipation. *Finally, I'm leaving the tensions of Antarctica behind.* But the moment she commenced the climb up the steep steps to board the aircraft, a flood of doubts blitzed her brain. She slowed her pace. *Do Kurt and the team know about the allegations made against me? And do I have the ornithological expertise they're expecting of me?*

Once on board, Kat found herself seated next to fellow ornithologist, Juan, to whom she'd first been introduced by Levi, at a New York conference. She wondered how she'd come to sit in the aisle seat beside him, knowing he and Athena had travelled together to the base.

"Hello, Juan. Where's Athena?" she enquired, checking out the passengers around her.

"Huh? Why?" he said with a snappy gruffness.

Kat flinched. "Oh … Oh, nothing really … I—"

Wow. This guy is super sensitive. They must have had a falling out.

Kat shrank down in her seat and turned her head the other way. The firm clunk of her locking seatbelt matched the immediate clamping of her lips. A tense silence ensued.

After take-off, Kat dared to snatch a quick peek past Juan and out the cabin window. The vast Antarctic landscape unveiled its frozen magic, bathed in the submerged sun's ghostly gloom. It was only the pilot's announcement of the estimated flight time to Punta Arenas airport, that finally broke Juan's frostiness.

"Nearly five hours," he mumbled. "Didn't think it would take that long."

Well at least he's talking to me now. Kat shifted back up in her seat.

"So where do we go after we land, Juan?"

"We'll be staying in Punta Arenas. Then next day we travel out to the king penguin colony. I'm told there's not enough accommodation for us all there, so we'll have to return the same day. … But on another note: are you still applying for Levi Stanton's position?"

Kat stiffened at his sudden digression.

"Ah … when it's advertised. Yes, I do want to apply. But I have some hurdles to overcome first."

"Hurdles?"

Her fingers dug into the arm rest. "Let's just say there was a scheming case of backstabbing at the base."

"Hmm … and I think I know where that came from. You know how rumours circulate in confined quarters."

He leaned across. "The ever scheming, Henri?" he whispered.

Kat nodded. "I won't say anymore because I know he's your friend."

"Friend? Henri? Hah, Henri's no friend of mine. That man just killed my friendship with Athena."

Should I press him? No, I won't. I'll give him some space. Bide my time. But maybe I've found myself an ally in the fight to clear my name.

The buffeting of the aircraft surfing a patch of blinding white cloud shook Kat from her lengthy snooze.

"Oh, we're here … already?" She sat upright in her seat.

"Not too long now til we land," said Juan, craning his neck to take in the views from the cabin window.

"Nice to see the sun again." She stretched out her arms and yawned, then surveyed the surprisingly arid landscape below.

The flight from Antarctica wasn't a commercial arrival. There was no comfortable jet-bridge gangway to protect the team from the ferocious force of the unrelenting Roaring Forties. As she stepped warily out the aircraft door, Kat was forced to grab the handrail. Then gripping it with both hands, she sidled down, one windblown step at a time.

After being fast tracked through the airport, the team members were shuttled to their accommodation. Along the route, Kurt pointed out the temporary Research Centre they had been granted use of.

"I'm sorry, Kat," Kurt apologised as the team assembled in the hotel lobby, "we don't have any single rooms. I'm afraid that means you'll have to share a twin room with one of us guys."

She cast her eyes over the team realising the only one she trusted was Juan.

"Don't worry, Kurt. In my line of work, I've often had to share a room during field assignments. I'll be happy, as long as the hotel has a gym."

He nodded. "Yes there is a small gym." He swatted his forehead. "Phew, I've been sweating on having to tell you about the accommodation situation."

Her eyes fixed on his unkempt beard. *Oh no, don't tell me he wants me to share with him.*

She was forced into thinking on her feet and piped up; "the team member I've come to know best is Juan. I'm happy to share with him—well that's if he'll have me."

Juan let out a chuckle. "Of course we can share a room, Kat."

The crease disappeared from her face.

That evening, as the team strolled the blustery deserted street to a nearby seafood restaurant, they were accosted by a strangely vocal man. Garbed in what appeared to be an old black oilskin coat, he was waving his arms and pointing toward the restaurant.

"What on Earth's he raving about? Do any of you know the local language?" asked Kurt.

Everyone returned a blank stare, apart from Juan.

"Don't know exactly, but it's something to do with fish. I thought he was saying: 'not to eat the fish,' or something like that. And in case you're wondering, I don't think he's been drinking."

They all filed into the gracious old wooden building, with its Victorian décor, crystal chandeliers and exquisite formally laid tables. For Kat, the establishment appeared more akin to something out of a ritzy precinct of London—that was until something got up her nose.

"Can you smell something … something musty?" she asked Juan.

"Mmm, know what you mean, there is a strange sort of staleness. But don't forget this is a very old building, and it's made of wood."

After perusing the menu, Juan whispered in Kat's ear. "I notice they do have mostly fish on the menu. To be honest, I have to wonder about the insistent way that man out there was attempting to get his message across. I got the impression he was trying to warn us. Maybe it'd be prudent to give the fish a miss until we find out more from the locals."

Kat pleaded with her eyes. "Please, Juan, you're the only one who managed to make some sense of the message the man was trying to get across. It's important you tell the team what you think. You must inform them. And perhaps we should dine at the hotel from now on."

Juan leaned into the table, cleared his throat, then addressed the team. He voiced a second discreetly hushed warning about what he thought he'd heard from the man ranting out on the street.

Kat detected a smirk of cynicism from a couple of team members, so she added her opinion. "You don't think the man was trying to tell us they might be disguising penguin meat as fish, do you?" said Kat, wriggling out her distaste.

Although she couldn't do any more than back Juan's warning, she held her breath every time a meal arrived from the kitchen.

Chapter Nineteen

Back at the Antarctic Base, Henri was busy packing his bags to fly home to New York. Despite the darkness outside, it was still autumn at the Pole, but he didn't want to run the risk of a winter-like burst of bad weather delaying his flight.

On the evening before his departure, Henri received a call from Kurt Matthews, detailing a disturbing spectacle the team had encountered at the king penguin colony just out of Punta Arenas. Having to investigate the same bizarre brain swelling in the king penguins as the Franklin Island emperors had proved distressing. But now the team reported a second more ominous phenomenon: a foreboding hint of calamity. They were shocked to discover thousands of dying fish washed up on the shoreline of the king colony.

Kat and the others in Kurt's team scooped up samples of the stricken fish and transported them back to the local Research Centre for evaluation.

On hearing the troubling news from Punta Arenas, Henri, in his egotistical drive for career recognition, immediately contacted the Senior Ornithologist at The Society's New York office. He informed the scientist of the team's gruesome discovery. But his face reddened on hearing The

Society had already heard about the fish crisis. Local news reporters on the ground in Punta Arenas had beaten him to what he'd assumed was his very own news scoop. When he discovered The Society had fully embraced the Punta Arenas local news leak, Henri's voice rose in anger.

"You mean to tell me you fell for a story reeled out by some lowly uneducated Chilean locals when you knew we had a team of experts on the ground in Punta Arenas. Are you all bird brains in there or something?"

His angry rant was met by deathly silence.

"Why in the hell do you think we invested valuable Society funding to dispatch a team to Chile? Didn't it occur to you, the story the press have jumped on might have been false?"

He allowed the scientist no time to respond.

"You do realise you've gone and inflicted a shit load of misery and food shortages on the world population." Henri huffed out an exasperated splutter then terminated the call.

The news leak from Punta Arenas locals made instant and frightening world headlines. The media release sparked unprecedented panic. A fear all southern hemisphere fish had been either poisoned or had succumbed to some mystery virus had the world gripped in mass hysteria.

Despite authorities urging a wait and see approach, a snowballing tide of unrest had already swept the globe. Millions were refusing to consume anything originating from the seas of the Southern Ocean. Fishmongers and supermarkets quickly withdrew and destroyed all seafood they considered might be contaminated. And just as Henri had predicted, the spectre of food shortages loomed large, especially for some of the poorer and more populated countries south of the equator.

For once, world leaders, even those who normally wouldn't entertain the idea of talking to each other, raced to Switzerland to attend a hastily convened summit. The objective: to share strategies for battling the mystery killer, and to pledge their country's foremost experts. But just as the big black limousines began pulling up outside the swanky Geneva venue, the worst possible news broke. Millions of dead fish had been discovered on the bountiful shores of the Galapagos Islands. The menacing nightmare of the killer phenomenon spreading north of the equator was now a reality. Just a few kilometres from the Galapagos Islands, lay the vast seas of the Northern Hemisphere.

Soon after take-off for New York, a voice from behind called out to Henri. He looked up to see Ben, pointing to the empty seat next to his. Like Henri and the other staff, Ben didn't want to be left stranded at the Pole over the long and gruelling darkness of winter.

"Would you mind if I sit next to you for a bit?" he asked, leaning over to look him in the eye. "I was hoping you might update me on how the team are going in Chile?"

Henri wriggled uncomfortably and lowered the middle arm rest. "Ah … yes, you can sit … well, for a while at least. But I am planning on stretching out soon."

"Of course," Ben assured him. "Just a quick catch up."

He clambered into the seat and buckled up.

"So, New York's your home, Henri?"

"I live and work in New York. What about you, where are you heading?"

"I'm aching to get home to my two daughters. They don't live far from you: White Plains—they stay with my Mom."

"Oh ..."

"Henri?" Ben's voice quavered. "I'm ..." There was a strange pause. "I'm wondering how long the team are going to be in Punta Arenas?"

Henri sat up straight in his seat. This was such an unanticipated question. He paused for a few seconds trying to fathom where the conversation might be going.

"As far as I can ascertain, they may be there for quite some time. You did hear about all those dying fish washing up at the king penguin colony near there?"

"I did. I guess they'll be kept busy trying to come up with an explanation for that."

"Very."

"Okay. Thanks, Henri. I'll get back to my seat now; let you stretch out. It's a long flight to Santiago."

Henri rolled his eyes as Ben bumbled back to his seat. "Damned idiot. What in the hell was that all about?" he muttered under his breath.

Chapter Twenty

As a bobbing blanket of rotting fish lay fouling their shoreline, the residents of Punta Arenas prayed their city's winds would remain in their prevailing offshore direction. Even the slightest deviation in wind trajectory whipped a putrid stench through the city.

While Kurt and his scientific team were busying themselves probing the reason for the king penguin brain swelling and the death of thousands of dead fish, an unlikely alliance of countries had begun deploying their pre-eminent scientists to the Galapagos Islands. This elite group of international academics aimed to find ways to cutail any threat to sea life in the Northern Hemisphere.

Although Kurt and his scientific team verified the king penguin brain swelling phenomenon was identical to that of the Franklin Island emperors, the same could not be said for the dying fish. None of the team on Franklin had ever stopped to consider venturing out to their island's distant and rocky shoreline at the time the emperors were afflicted. Had they done so, they may well have witnessed the same foreboding sight in Antarctic waters.

For Kat, the unexpectedly prolonged stint in Punta Arenas was proving challenging in more ways than one. Sharing a room with Juan was becoming unbearable. During the last two nights she'd awoken to the thwack of his dirty socks and soiled clothing landing on her face—retaliation for her snoring keeping him awake. However, his actions only made her plight worse. She said nothing on the first morning. But during the day she struggled with tiredness and grumpiness from lack of sleep. Following a second bad night, she resolved to confront him when they arrived home from the Research Centre.

After taking a shower at around five in the afternoon, Kat sat Juan down before they headed out to dinner. From the sound of his fingers tapping the arm of the chair, she figured he wasn't happy.

"I didn't say anything yesterday, Juan, but throwing your dirty socks and underwear at me during the night is not on. I'm not putting up with behaviour like that."

He looked away.

"Listen, I know I have bouts of snoring. Don't we all?" She raised her voice, "and believe it or not, you do too."

"But your snoring's so loud it keeps me awake."

"Okay, okay. I apologise. But there has to be a more civilised way of alerting me. How would you like it if I threw the cleaning cloths I use every morning to wipe up the urine dribble you leave around the toilet every night?"

"What! What are you talking about?"

"Juan, I'm talking about your lack of aim in the small hours of the night."

"Rubbish!" he sneered with a bang of his fist on the armrest. He scrambled to his feet and stormed out.

Only seconds after, there was a knock at the door.

Bet he's back to apologise.

Kat opened the door expecting a face of remorse. But she exhaled a gasp.

"Ben! What are you doing here?"

"Was that Juan who just ran out the door?"

"Ah … yes."

"Oh." His gaze darted to the floor. "Are you two…?"

"No! No way. We've been forced into sharing this room, but we're not getting along. I'm not enjoying slumming it with him at all."

Ben surveyed the two beds, taking in the unmistakable division of both their bedclothes and their personal items.

"Phew, that's a relief. I thought you'd fallen for a younger man."

"Hah, I'm old enough to be Juan's mother." She let out a giggle. "I just did the motherly confrontation thing about the mess he makes in the bathroom." She lowered her voice. "The guy won't admit he can't aim straight. That's why he ran from the room."

Ben grinned. They stood for a moment, staring into one another's eyes.

"I thought you said you were going home to spend time with your daughters."

"I … I got as far as Rio … and, oh Kat, I haven't stopped thinking about you."

Without warning, he reached into his pocket and dipped down at her feet. "Sorry, I'm not the world's most romantic man, but I've bought you this." His trembling fingers prized open a small red velvet covered box. "I've spent my every waking moment thinking about you, Kat. Will you marry me?"

She ogled the sparkling diamond then looked into his clear blue eyes. A whirl of emotions flashed through her head. *I do have to admit I've missed him. Am I ever going to find anyone else at my age?*

After a moment of contemplation, she responded.

"Ben, this comes as a bit of a shock. I mean, we haven't even dated yet. But yes, I am keen to get to know you better. I'd like it if we can start in a more romantic way. How about we meet at the hotel restaurant for dinner tonight? I can introduce you to any of the team you haven't met, then we can do the town after dinner. Our very first date."

Although unhappy sharing with Juan, the question Kat had to mull over was whether to endure the tension between them or move in with Ben. Despite feeling no pressure from him to cohabit, her past hurt continued to haunt her. The unrelenting fear of rejection kept flashing through her mind. She battled to erase the pain of finding a strange woman in her one and only lover's bed. She ruminated about which way to turn. *I do want to get to know Ben better before I make a final commitment, but...*

The long-awaited results of the autopsies on the Punta Arenas dying fish were ready for release to the world later the same morning Ben arrived in town. Kurt Matthews had agreed to a media conference to announce the team's findings. As the team pulled up outside the local broadcasting building, a small goods proprietor was busily boarding up his shopfront on the other side of the road.

"Are we in for a hurricane or something?" said Kurt, surveying the scene.

Juan darted across the road to ask the shop owner what he was doing. The man raised his voice and raged at him. Juan stood his ground taking the venom. He then dashed back across to the team who'd slinked up the steps and into the entryway of the broadcasting building.

"What's he so angry about?" Kurt enquired.

"The man's blaming us for his grocery store being looted–" He paused for a moment to catch his breath. "Said something about us scaring people into not eating fish. He said a group of teens were so hungry, they mobbed together, overpowered him, and pillaged his store."

Little did the team know this apocalyptic scenario had begun flaring throughout the South American continent. Even more disturbing, out of control youths engaging in copycat incidents had been wreaking havoc in the northern hemisphere.

The team were escorted to the media room, where Kurt was to present a detailed account of the findings they'd identified at the local Research Centre.

As they began taking their seats around the long rectangular table, one of the English-speaking staff entered the room and interrupted the proceedings.

"Can you confirm for me?" he asked, his eyes skimming the room, "whether all your team are here this morning? You're not missing anyone, are you?"

Kurt gazed around the table, giving his team the once-over. "No. We're not missing a soul. I can definitely confirm all my team are here. Why do you ask?"

"Our local police have just issued an incident statement. A man has been admitted to intensive care after being attacked in the street. His wallet and ID have been stolen, but from his clothing and footwear labels, they think he may be a US or Canadian national."

Chapter Twenty-One

Kurt Matthews and his team were unprepared for the arrogant and predatory manner of the news correspondent fronting the local media conference. The man's beady eyes glared each of them down before the cameras began rolling. He then hit them with an oddball initial question, demanding to know how the results of their research could possibly help save the world's multibillion dollar fish farming industry.

Fortunately for the team, Kurt maintained his usual composed manner. After empathising over the increasing losses of the world's fish stocks and its millions of panicked consumers, he digressed to outline the scientific achievements his team had made at the Punta Arenas Research Centre. But to his bewilderment, he was rudely interrupted.

"I think the world's more anxious to know what differences there were between what happened to the penguins on Franklin Island, and what hit the birds right here in Chile," he harped.

"Of course. And it's on my schedule." Kurt tapped his paperwork. "I will be getting to it as quickly as I can."

He then went on to discuss the one big discovery the world needed to be told.

"With the mystery pathogen having spread so uncontrollably, we're heartened by the fact that to date, there have been no more human deaths since the Antarctic team succumbed. That's extremely reassuring when we're dealing with a virus we've never encountered before."

"And can you explain why? Why there would be no more human casualties?" the interviewer asked.

"Our research has been focused entirely on penguins, and this is because we know the Antarctic team consumed penguin meat. But we're certain other fish-eating birds and mammals have been exposed to the virus. Yet, so far, not another single human death has been reported."

"So, you're implying humans eat seals and other marine mammals?"

Kurt looked to the ceiling. "Yes, that's exactly what I'm saying. We believe many remote indigenous peoples continue to consume marine mammal meat."

"What you're preaching then is, white western people don't consume mammal meat from the sea? Isn't that rather a racist perception?"

Kurt wriggled with exasperation. Kat half expected him to stand to his feet and storm out. "Those are your words. Not mine."

The interviewer paused momentarily, continuing to feign his smug expression.

"I'm sure the people of Punta Arenas and Chile are keen to know what else your team discovered on our shores."

Kurt was quick to draw a parallel to the massing behaviour of the local king penguins and those of the Franklin Island emperors. "Also," he added, "the fish appeared to cluster at the shoreline to die. What I'm saying is, while this congregating behaviour is comparable to the gathering of the Franklin emperors, it was also evident in the deceased Antarctic team. Oh, and by the way, Katrina

Ingledew, their leader is with us here today, she can confirm how she experienced the same phenomenon in her team."

"The Franklin Island team leader? Here, in this room? Why's she– ?"

"Aah … please allow me to finish. I need to tell you Kat experienced considerable distress attempting to get her team to evacuate the station. And we must remember, she was the only member who didn't consume penguin meat. What I was about to say was, the fact the deceased members were found grouped in one room when they were discovered, replicates exactly the pre-death rituals observed in both the dying penguins and the fish. We have a real mystery on our hands."

"Okay, you've covered that similarity. Now our viewers will be curious to know how your only Franklin Island survivor ended up working in our Punta Arenas Research Centre after being charged with abandoning her team."

Kurt paused for a moment, temporarily dumbfounded by the audacity of the question.

"I heard you say charged. Are you aware the word charged, doesn't equate to being judged guilty?"

With that, Kurt bundled up his paperwork, straightening each side of the stack on his desk with a solid thud. He then calmly announced he and the team had provided all the information they had prepared for the interview and needed to press on with their research at the Centre.

After the team exited the building, Juan apologised to Kurt for the bad manners of the interviewer.

"That guy was an arrogant prick. I don't know how you kept your cool. He made me ashamed to admit I have South American roots, as well as Mexican."

"You've no need to apologise, Juan. But I do agree with your opinion of the man."

Later in the day, after finishing work, Kat and Juan found themselves back in their room at the hotel. He flopped straight into one of the armchairs and motioned Kat to join him.

"Wow, it's been quite a day hasn't it, Kat?" he said, kicking off his shoes. "The proprietor having to board up his shop was shock enough, but wasn't that interviewer something else?"

Kat leaned further back in her chair in a discreet move to avoid the pong of his socks. Plus, she wasn't in the mood for small talk. Juan must have picked up on her coolness. He began fidgeting, undoing his top two shirt buttons then broke into an edgy rambling about his regret over what took place between them early that morning.

"Sorry I flared up on you this morning. I'm not a morning person. I can't handle *anything* at that hour. Hey, that reminds me, I'm positive I caught a glimpse of someone I knew from the base out in the hallway when I left this morning. I thought it was… Hey, that guy Ben's not here in Punta Arenas is he?"

"Yes, that was Ben. He'd checked in at reception after an early morning flight. He was on his way up to see me."

"Of course. He was the rescue pilot. I thought it was him."

"He's joining us for a meal here at the hotel restaurant tonight."

Dinners in the hotel restaurant were becoming tedious for Kat. She'd tried every main on the menu more than twice. Although the service and food were impeccable, her face lit up whenever Kurt and the team chose to dine out at other eateries. But there was always the same end of the working week routine: Kurt insisted on the hotel restaurant for Friday nights. She assumed it was so they wouldn't have to walk the streets after a few drinks.

As she always did, Kat stooped to savour the scent-laden perfume of the roses adorning the ornate vases at the entrance to the restaurant.

"How do they manage to grow such magnificent roses in such a rugged climate?" she'd asked the first time she caught the heady scent of their bouquet.

As the team made their way to their table, she scanned the room for Ben. *Where is he? I told him I'd book him in for tonight.*

She pulled out her chair, placing her handbag on the seat next to her.

"Expecting another diner?" asked the waiter as he hovered beside her at the table.

"Um–" she froze at the expectant look on everyone's faces. "There is another gentleman joining me tonight."

"Ooooh," a concerted chorus rang out as their eyes fixed on her flushing face.

"I'm sure you'll all remember Ben, the helicopter pilot who was stationed at the base."

"A special date, eh?" said Kurt with a cheeky smile.

Kat pretended to peruse the menu.

As the minutes passed, a sinking sensation weighed in her stomach. *I hope I didn't hurt his feelings with my dating suggestion. What if he's taken it as a rejection and is on his way back to New York?*

Kat ordered from the menu then quickly excused herself. "Sorry, I'm wondering if I've given Ben the wrong time. I'll just do a quick check to see if he's still in his room."

The hotel receptionist phoned his room while she waited.

"Sorry ma'am. He's not picking up."

"He hasn't vacated his room, has he?"

"The room's still in his name."

"Thank you for checking. If he comes through the doors, can you let him know we're waiting for him in the restaurant." *Bet he's gone out to buy me flowers. That'd be Ben.*

Kat trotted back to the restaurant, head in the air, beaming with the knowledge Ben was still around and would turn up any minute. She hoped he might excuse his delay with flowers, or some other first date present he might have gone out to buy.

By the time her meal arrived, Kat's face was furrowed with disappointment.

Juan checked the time. "So, Ben wasn't in his room?"

"No. He must have gone out. I can't even contemplate where he might be."

Kurt overheard their conversation. "I take it he is staying at this hotel?"

"Yes, I asked at reception. He's definitely still checked in."

"Oh, no …" Kurt murmured. "Sorry, I'd forgotten. You know that guy who came into the media room at the studio this morning? Didn't he say a man had been attacked in the street? Something about him being in intensive care.

I'm sure he said the police thought he might be an American or Canadian."

A spine-chilling silence numbed the room.

Chapter Twenty-Two

On his first day back at Head Office in New York, Henri was rattled to find, in his extended absence, a younger colleague, had taken over deceased President, Levi Stanton's role in administering the day-to-day running of The World Ornithological Society. To add to his woes, he received a call to appear before the Executive Board at 9am the very next morning. This caused him to wallow in a mire of sinking dread. His anxiety became so paralysing, he signed off for the day, citing the fatigue effect of jetlag after his non-stop flight from Rio de Janeiro to New York.

On his early commute home from work, Henri agonised over what excuse he might offer at tomorrow's inquiry.

I'm betting they'll accuse me of an unnecessary stay over in Rio. They're going to say I exploited my position.

He began thinking up valid reasons to justify taking his break. Oh, to hell with them. He drummed his fingers on his briefcase. *I spent way too long in the Antarctic with no sunlight. I'll tell them it spiralled me into a depressive mood. I'll tell them I'm still suffering from being forced to stay so long down there. And it's true. Most of my time was spent in twenty-four-hour darkness.*

Despite his resolve to put forward a valid excuse for his Brazilian sojourn, Henri tossed and turned through the night. Fears of persecution hounded his psyche.

The Board have already made up their mind who they want in Levi's position. I knew that the minute I saw that young upstart planted in Levi's office. They're out to bypass me, I know it.

Next morning, Henri made a point of arriving at work at eight sharp. He ended up sitting forlorn in his office. *Something's brewing. Not one member of staff wants to strike up a conversation with me. No one's even bothered to come to my door to ask how I'm coping after going home sick yesterday.*

When he heard his name called, Henri jumped to his feet, anxious to get the dreaded ordeal over and done with. He hightailed his escort to the board room. As he walked in, he bowed his head to avoid the snarl of staring faces.

Henri froze the minute the board commenced their questioning. The subject of their enquiry slammed him, catching him by surprise. Henri was so flabbergasted by the board leader's accusatory prattle, the man's words jumbled his brain.

"The World Ornithological Society was represented by you as its leader. You were there on the spot in Antarctica, Henri. Yet you failed to warn the Franklin Island team about the dangers of consuming penguin meat."

Trickles of sweat ran down his chest. And the condemnations kept on coming.

"You were right there. Why didn't you arrange to get those team members out to safety?"

"I …" He stalled, momentarily lost for words. His face reddened and his body tremored.

"What? What is it you want to say?" the chief executive demanded. "All we're asking is, why didn't you make more of an effort to assist the team down there? You, above all people, were fully aware of the gravity of their situation. That's the very reason we sent you down there."

Henri shuffled to straighten his posture. "Well, you obviously have no idea what really transpired on Franklin Island," he retorted. "The team leader, Kat Ingledew—she tried her darnedest to talk her members into taking the rescue option at the same time she did."

"We are aware of that. But you were in charge. It was your responsibility to intervene. You should have insisted on going in and warning them about the danger of remaining at the station. You knew full well they were running out of supplies."

"I did try. I remember shouting with anger when I saw Kat climbing aboard the helicopter without the rest of her team. And I had a go at her about it when she returned to the base."

Henri's bluster was met with silence.

"Okay then," he huffed. "I'll get Katrina Ingledew to back up my side of the story. She'll readily confirm her team's defiance."

After leaving the meeting Henri slunk back to his office and closed the door.

"Damn it." He smacked his palm on his forehead. "I was the one who dobbed Kat into the Australian authorities for abandoning her team. Now I'm the one being blamed. How the hell am I ever going to get her to back me up?"

He sat scowling at the peering eyes and the hasty head turns as staff skulked by his window.

I'm sure Kat and I can work to present a united front. It'll get us both off the hook. Yes, I'll get in touch with her and apologise.

The minute he arrived home from work, Henri messaged Juan, the only person he had contact details for in the Punta Arenas team. When he divulged the situation he'd been confronted with by the Society's Board, he frowned at the terse reply he received.

'Hey Henri, there's a hell of a lot going on for us down here right now. Please contact me again tomorrow evening.'

Henri's phone landed with a thud on the sofa. *A lot going on. What in the hell does he mean by that?*

Chapter Twenty-Three

The fear of global food shortages was no longer just a fear. Panic over the rampaging marine virus rapidly escalated. In populations dependent on the ocean's bounty, the grim reaper of famine was now an ugly reality. For the hungry masses in the densely populated Southern Hemisphere cities of South America and Africa, riots had become a daily occurrence. The fight for survival had society devolving to its lowermost human condition: every person for himself.

Although the Northern Hemisphere was now basking in summer warmth, there'd been no forewarning of food shortages—no time to prepare or plant the compensatory food crops, or to raise the extra animals required to sustain the seething masses of the world's burgeoning mega cities.

From the sanctuary of his cushy office tower, Henri tensed at the sound of the increasingly ominous wail of police and fire sirens in the streets below. Uncontrollable looting and lawlessness had begun to plague the city he so loved. His heart raced when he witnessed the first of many plumes of smoke billowing skywards from nearby fires. He reeled at news reports of starving youths venting their anger by torching empty stores in some parts of the city. The starving masses on the streets below had nothing to lose. Sadly, for

New York, it was nothing more than panic buying that had triggered food prices to more than treble.

Henri attempted to contact Juan again, but his efforts were stymied by an inexplicable communications failure. After witnessing the looting rampage in the streets surrounding his tower, he concluded it would be safer to overnight in his office and keep trying to reach him.

Thousands of miles due south, in Punta Arenas, Kurt Matthew's speculation the victim of a local street mugging may have been Ben, cast an unsettling tension over his team at dinner.

"I've got to go. What if it is Ben?" Kat cried, pushing her chair back as she shot up from the table.

"I'll come with you," said Juan, you can't go walking out there alone at this hour."

"Can you tell us where the hospital is?" Juan asked one of the waiting staff as they made their way to the exit.

"Go around the hotel corner, then next street on the left. Only a five-minute walk."

"C'mon let's go." He hooked Kat's arm in his and escorted her out onto the street.

Kat shivered at the frigid winter air biting her skin. *It can't be Ben. It can't be. I'm going to see his smiling face coming toward me any minute now.* She loosened her arm from Juan's, pretending she needed to adjust her scarf. But as they turned the corner, she realised her hope of running into Ben wasn't going to happen.

As they lengthened their stride, a vrooming roar from a vehicle thundered behind them. Kat turned her head to see a car mounting the pavement and heading straight for them.

"Juan. Look out!" She grabbed his arm and pulled him to her. But a clunky thud walloped her ears as the vehicle smacked his body. He was knocked off balance and landed with a sickening whomp on the hard pavement. Juan slowly raised himself, first on one elbow, then onto all fours. He began rubbing his shoulder.

"I'm okay, I'm okay," he whimpered.

The vehicle pulled up in the shadows up ahead, its engine ticking over.

He pointed up the street. "That's the one."

But as soon as he stumbled to his feet, it sped away, tyres squealing and smoke pouring from the rear.

"Oh, Juan," Kat cried. "You need an ambulance."

"No, no, I'm just bruised. I think the wing mirror slammed me in the shoulder. Honest, I'm fine. More sore from the fall. But I dread to think what would have happened if you hadn't pulled me out of the way." He reached out his hand for support. "Let's go. I can see the hospital lights glowing in the distance."

With Kat's arm supporting his waist, he began hobbling toward the building.

When they reached the hospital entrance, Kat darted in and begged for urgent medical assistance. She hovered at Juan's side as he was wheeled into emergency and checked over.

"Nothing broken, I'm pleased to report," said Doctor Ariko, an English-speaking physician.

"You can dress now, but you'll be a bit sore and bruised for a few days. I should warn you, a gang of thugs has been targeting tourists in the hotel and restaurant precinct. There's a lot of aggro over food shortages. Best to keep off the streets."

"It's a coincidence you should mention that," said Juan. He turned to Kat. "Ben's from the US isn't he?"

She nodded.

"Kat and I were on our way here to ask about the victim of a serious assault. Do you know anything about a male assault victim being admitted?"

"I do know about the gentleman you're enquiring after. You are … family, I take it?"

"No, not family. But a friend of Kat's didn't show up for dinner tonight. She's very worried it may be him–"

"Yes," Kat interrupted, "I've worked with him."

"I'm afraid the victim's still in a coma. His wallet and any other ID he may have had are missing. We have no way of identifying him."

"Have you seen him then?" Kat enquired.

"No. I only know he's Caucasian and probably in his late thirties, maybe early forties."

She chewed her lip.

Juan sensed her distress and stepped in. "As we think we might know him, is it possible we'd be able to see him? Hopefully we can rule out he isn't our friend."

"I can arrange for you to see him, but I'm afraid this facility has a rule of only one person at a time at intensive care patients' bedsides."

Kat and Juan eyed each other, their faces lined with uncertainty.

"Probably best you go in, Kat," Juan suggested. "You know Ben a lot better than I do. I'll take a seat in the waiting area."

With a heavy gulp, she shadowed the doctor to the ward, her heart racing all the way.

Kat pinched in the top of her medical mask as she entered the ward.

"The gentleman in question's in the bed right at the very end." The doctor pointed the way.

She held her breath in an attempt to quell the flapping in her stomach.

When they reached the bed, the curtains were pulled around, but a slight waft revealed activity behind.

"Looks as though one of the nurses is in there. We'll have to wait."

With legs turning to jelly, Kat looked around for a chair. But there was nowhere to sit to relieve her surging nausea.

When the front curtain was finally swished back, a doctor emerged and gestured the all-clear to enter.

Kat uttered a mournful cry as she flew to the bedside. Despite the gaggle of tubes braiding his face, she exhaled a gasp of recognition.

"It *is* him," She cried. "It's definitely my friend, Ben."

Her eyes teared up as she hovered over his comatose body.

"Oh, Ben … Ben. Can I touch his hand?"

"Of course you can. You can even hold his hand if you like," the doctor counselled, standing well back. "I'm going to leave you for a few minutes to go and chase up Doctor Garcia, who was just in with him. He'll be able to tell us more about his condition and prognosis."

Kat stood at the bedside clutching Ben's cool pale hand.

Oh, why didn't I accept your offer to fly to White Plains and meet your daughters? This wouldn't have happened if you hadn't had to follow me here.

"Oh Ben, please come back to me," she whispered in his ear. "I'm so sorry for what's happened. You're the sweetest guy. I really did mean it when I said I wanted you to romance me into a marriage proposal. More than anything in the world, I want to find a man I can trust. It was only the betrayal from my past that's left me frightened to commit again—"

Her heart-wrenching whisperings were interrupted by the curtain being opened and the two doctors returning to the bedside.

"This is Doctor Garcia," said Doctor Ariko. "I'm going to translate for you—everything he's informed me about your friend's condition, and his likely prognosis. If you should have any questions, I can put them to him."

Kat gulped at the formality, and their gloomy faces. She braced for the details.

"Doctor Garcia says the attack was brutal in the extreme. He was as good as left for dead. There is traumatic brain injury. But the good news is, his chance of recovering from the coma is reasonable. But if he does survive, it's likely there'll be long lasting consequences. Doctor Garcia is hopeful he'll come around in the next two or three days. Then he'll run tests, and we'll know more.

Ben's bleak prognosis left Kat quivering. She couldn't think of anything more to ask.

"Oh, and by the way," Doctor Ariko added. "Doctor Garcia also informed me there was one reliable eyewitness to the assault. Yes, a woman sitting in a wheelchair at the window of a second-floor apartment above. She observed the final moments of the beating. Strangely, it wasn't the local thugs I warned you about earlier. The woman claimed the perpetrators were three Caucasian males dressed in black business suits."

Chapter Twenty-Four

Kat jumped as the blue cubicle curtains flew open behind her. The duty nurse tapped the fob watch on her uniform.

Oh no, it feels as though I've only just sat down with Ben.

"Thank you, nurse. I'll leave you to your…" Her whisper faltered as she rose from his bedside.

"I wanted to stay longer with Ben, but he's on limited visiting time," she blubbered on her return to Juan, who was sitting alone in the dimly lit gloom of the waiting area.

He jumped up, reached out and wrapped her in his arms. "That's understandable," he said, his breath warm on her neck. "Especially when he's in a coma."

Kat was reluctant to leave the cocoon of Juan's hug. She held on for as long as he permitted.

"How about we go back to the hotel and have a bite to eat. Don't forget, we missed out on dinner. Are you hungry?"

"Not really." Her face flushed at the intensity of her need for his embrace. She took a step back. "But you must be famished, Juan. And I suppose I need some sustenance in this freezing climate."

"C'mon then, let's go." He held out his hand.

"But shouldn't we take a taxi after what happened out there earlier?"

"Nah, just take my hand. We'll fly." He looked right, then left, then to Kat. "Yeah, let's make a run for it."

By the time Juan and Kat reached their hotel, they were panting. He requested a table for two and they ordered.

"What would you like to drink, Kat? I don't know about you, but I'm in the mood to celebrate." He punched his fist in the air. "Hey, I survived an attempt on my life today. I'm here to live another day."

She squirmed at his insensitivity toward Ben. "Yes, a stiff drink thanks. Maybe a scotch and ice."

While Juan feasted on a large supper, Kat picked at the meagre salad on her plate.

"Another scotch please, Juan." A big one.

The dining conversation floated from a sharing of experiences in their fields of work, to their horror at the apocalyptic famine rampaging the globe. Not a word about Ben, or the tragedy to which he'd succumbed was uttered.

When a smartly uniformed Chilean waitress began hovering, Juan took the hint. It was time to head to their room.

"What? Closing time already?" Kat looked up to see the waitress grinning.

"Oh, so it is." said Juan, acknowledging her subtle prompt.

Kat stumbled as she rose from the table. Her tittering giggle had Juan rushing to assist.

"Sorry, I overindulged. It's been a hell of a day," she said as he took her arm.

When Juan opened the hotel room door, Kat walked in and burst into tears.

"Oh, Kat, Kat …" he murmured.

"It was here. It was right here," she cried. "It was only hours ago that Ben surprised me with an engagement ring."

Juan gaped. "Oh …"

"Yes, if only I'd accepted his proposal and worn the ring … none of this would have happened."

"What? You mean you turned him down?"

"No. I told him I wanted to be romanced first," she sobbed. "You know—like dated. I'm certain he was mugged on his way to buy me flowers, or chocolates, or … something."

"That's the reason then …" he asked with doleful eyes.

"What do you mean?"

"Why you drowned you sorrows tonight. And here was I thinking …"

"Thinking what?"

"It doesn't matter. I had no idea you and Ben were… dating."

As Juan contemplated Kat's tearful disclosure, his phone rang. It was Henri, but the reception was muffled.

"Juan! At last. I've been trying to get a hold of you. Is Kat at your hotel tonight? I need to talk to her. It's urgent."

"Sorry, Henri. Kat's not in a good space right now."

"What does *he* want?" she mouthed.

Juan shook his head and raised his palm. "How's it going in the Big Apple?" he asked, in an attempt to divert his demand.

"To be honest, I'm fearing for my life. I'm scared to go out on the street. I can't even get home. There's angry mobs out there … muggings, knifings, shootings … so much anger and violence. The gangs are setting fire to all the empty supermarkets as a protest."

"You're not alone, Henri. I came within an inch of being mown down by a car this evening. And you remember Ben, the helicopter pilot? He's in hospital in a coma after a vicious street attack. He was left for dead. He'll be lucky to survive."

The line suddenly cut out. "Oh no. Lost him."

"If he rings back, can you ask why he wants to talk to me?"

A few minutes later, as Kat emerged from the bathroom towelling her hair, Henri phoned again.

"Henri. Kat wants to know why you need to talk to her."

"Put her on," he insisted.

"Hello," Kat snapped. "You wanted to talk to me, Henri?"

"Yes, I need to ask a favour of you, Kat. I need you to be my witness. The Society's Executive Board have accused me of failing in my duty to ensure the Franklin Island team were rescued from the station. Listen, I've informed them you tried to get them to follow you out when you were rescued. I told them they refused your command. Do you remember how I had a go at you when you returned without them? That's all I need from you. To inform them of those two facts."

Kats fists clenched as she listened to his audacious request.

"Yes!" she snarled. "I remember all right. And you didn't believe me. Then you reported me to the Australian authorities. Now I'm facing charges the minute I step foot into Sydney airport."

"I know, I know. I did go too far. But what I'm saying is, if you help me out here, I'll do the same for you—I'll get you off the hook."

Kat stiffened. Her anger for the man fired up.

"I'm going to have to sleep on this, Henri."

"Eh? But … but—"

"No! I just told you. Leave it with me. I'll get back to you. I need to think about it." She terminated the call.

Later in the evening, as she lay in bed, heart racing, and brooding over her tumultuous day, Kat ruminated on the strange remark Juan made earlier about her drowning her sorrows.

Hmm, I've just figured it out. He assumed there was another reason I was drinking so much tonight. He thought I'd fall into bed with him when we got back to our room.

Chapter Twenty-Five

"Thanks for being so understanding," said Kat, when Kurt Matthews offered the green light to visit Ben anytime she wanted during working hours. Although she wasn't sure, she suspected Juan may have confided in him, telling Kurt of their plans to marry.

The very next morning, Kat visited Ben's bedside on her way to work. She hoped he would hear her comforting words of love and reassurance. But at the back of her mind, she harboured the agonising dread he might never wake up. How she longed to tell him he was the only man who'd ever managed to turn around her deep-rooted trust issues.

The sprawl of breathing and feeding tubes and the robotic beeping no longer spooked her. Once again, she caressed his hand and whispered words of reassurance. But she sighed on hearing the squeaky shoes of a duty nurse approaching. Her fleeting fifteen minutes was over. She looked up to find this duty nurse was new to her. And she shone a kindly smile.

"Do you speak any English?" Kat enquired.

"I did a five-year stint in London, so I took a giant step up with my English." Her smiling eyes eased Kat's trembling. "Anyway, my name's Elena. Is there something you'd like to ask?"

"I … I just don't know what to do … you know, how to make Ben more comfortable."

"You don't need to do anything. Just be here for him, my lovely. And keep talking to him. His brain may be aware. In which case he might hear you."

Kat's eyes teared up. "Really? Thanks. I'm hoping so."

After a very welcome five minutes more whispering to Ben, she headed off to work, a spring in her step, her head humming with the positive words of the kind-hearted Elena.

Kat waltzed into work to a buzz of speculation. Kurt was scheduled to make an official announcement just prior to lunch. A heavy dread weighed in the pit of her stomach.

I bet he's about to tell us our time here's up. But how can I leave? No. I would never leave Ben here on his own. Never.

Her work morning dragged. She contemplated the local employment opportunities—what might be available on completion of her current assignment. Her thoughts veered to the charges she would face should she have to return to Sydney. Fear of arrest made her even more thankful she might be able to stay on in Punta Arenas.

But what about Henri, and his offer to clear me of the charges if I do the same for him? Oh, all this uncertainty's getting too much.

At 11.30 sharp, Kurt called the team into the Research Centre's cramped meeting room. From the craggy lines crimping his forehead, Kat guessed the speculation of the project's end was correct.

"You'll all be wondering why I've called such an impromptu meeting. And believe me it has come out of the blue. I have some, well … good news. But I'm afraid I also received some dire news this morning from the World Health Organisation. I'm afraid the predicament we've all been fearing has struck us hard. Yes." He wiped his brow. "The first recorded cases of the virus jumping from marine life to humans has been reported in British Columbia, Canada. This news is grave in the extreme. Deaths followed only five days later."

A piercing silence numbed the room.

"This morning's call from WHO requested we ready ourselves to commit to further research. It's to our combined professional credit they want some of the proposed research to continue at this Centre. Now I realise you'll be anxious to spend time with your families before we commence a new undertaking, so I'm pleased to tell you that can be arranged immediately."

Surprisingly, there were few questions from the wide-eyed team. Not one team member requested to end their contract.

"I definitely won't be flying home to Sydney for a short break," said Kat, as she and Juan exited the meeting room. "What about you, Juan?"

"My family live in San Diego, but this time of year they visit relatives in Mexico. So probably not."

Kat chose to call into the hospital and sit with Ben on her way home from work. Juan had nothing else on, so he said he was happy to sit out in the waiting area.

As they approached the intensive care unit, Doctor Ariko came bounding through the doors, his face beaming.

"Good news! Good news! Your friend's showing signs of coming out of his coma. He opened his eyes and was even blinking. Even though it was only for a minute or so, it's a positive sign for his recovery, especially this early. And even more encouraging, the duty nurse confirmed he appeared to demonstrate a reasonable sense of awareness."

Kat couldn't help herself. She flung her arms around him, thanking him profusely. As she stepped back, Juan began chuckling, obviously amused at her burst of exuberance.

Kat's time with Ben grew even more vital now he'd demonstrated some degree of alertness. She made full use of her fifteen minutes with hushed murmurings of reassuring words. She stroked his pale hand in the hope he might respond. And she buzzed with contentment knowing he was in recovery mode.

Conversation at the team's hotel dinner that evening, centred around Ben's improving condition and the viral outbreak crisis gripping the globe. But the latest update, which Kurt received in the late afternoon, proved a disappointing blow to the team members hoping for a short break with their loved ones. After everyone was seated, Kurt broke the disheartening news.

"I know I promised you earlier in the day you'd be welcome to spend some time with your families before we commence our new project. I'm afraid the news I received this afternoon makes my promise virtually impossible. Travel between most countries has been suspended with immediate effect."

An outcry of disappointed 'ohs' rang out around the table.

Kurt shook his head. "Yes, and because this is global consensus, it really does confirm the extreme danger the world is facing. It's highly likely no-one has any resistance to fighting off this new virus. Our role here will be crucial in the investigations for a possible vaccine."

The relief of knowing Ben was on the way to recovery, eased Kat's anxiety and she fell into a deep sleep as soon as her head hit the pillow. But something disturbed her in the early hours of the morning. She sat bolt upright and tilted her head toward the window. The wailing of sirens grew louder and louder. There were multiple sirens, and they screamed on and on. The beating of her heart pounded her chest. She held her breath, listening for any sign of Juan being disturbed. But there was nothing. She lay back down and after a brief period of restlessness, managed to fall back to sleep.

"Did you hear all those sirens in the night?" Kat asked Juan as he emerged from his morning shower.

"Sirens? No, never heard a thing. What time was it?"

"When I checked, it was 1.20 am. They wailed on and on. But I did eventually get back to sleep."

"Nope. Nothing woke me. I slept like the proverbial baby."

"Well, there must have been something major going on out there."

Kat jumped at finding Juan right outside the door as she exited the bathroom. He took two steps back and froze on the spot.

"Did you hear the knock at our door just then?"

"No. I had the water running. Why?"

"That was Kurt doing the rounds. You're not going to believe this—those sirens you heard last night. He came to let us know the Research Centre's been burnt to the ground."

"Whaaat?!"

"Yes, it's true. Kurt said there's nothing left. The entire Centre's gone. Razed. Kaput. We're out of work and we can't even leave town. We're stranded."

Chapter Twenty-Six

Just seconds after Kat recoiled at the disastrous news Juan had divulged, his phone rang.

"Oh, what now?" he cussed, fumbling to pick it up.

Kat closed her eyes and turned away, dreading what other bad news might hit them next.

"It's Henri, calling again from New York. He wants to speak to you." He motioned Kat to take the phone.

Oh no not again. Well, at least he doesn't have my number. She pulled a face as she snatched the phone from Juan.

"Yes," she snapped.

"Kat! I'm still waiting for an answer on the offer I made you. Why haven't you contacted me?"

"Barely had time to think here, Henri. Our Research Centre was burnt to the ground last night. Just as we've commenced working toward a vaccine. We're all devastated. Weeks of dedicated research up in smoke. And with the global aviation shutdown, we're stuck here in Punta Arenas with no jobs."

Henri blew out an exaggerated sigh.

"Yes, and on top of all that, Henri—do you remember Ben, the helicopter pilot from the Base? He was beaten to a pulp and left for dead in a street near here. He's been in a coma ever since."

"A coma? Just as well he's a bit on the porky side then. That should sustain him until he comes around."

"Ooooh!" Kat threw the phone down on Juan's bed.

Juan stiffened. "What the hell was that all about?"

"Oh, the idiot. He made the most crass comment about Ben's weight."

"Eh?"

"Oh, it doesn't matter. But it's the sort of inappropriate rudeness I'd expect from Henri. If he calls back, I don't want to talk to him. And please don't, under any circumstances, give him my number."

"Your friend has made a remarkable recovery," said Doctor Ariko, his face beaming as he led Kat to Ben's bedside.

Seeing Ben with his eyes open and even recognising her, more than made up for her horror morning.

"So wonderful to have you back with me," she whispered, squeezing his hand in hers.

He blinked his eyes.

She turned to the doctor and whispered. "Has he been able to talk yet?"

"No. But I'm sure that will come."

Ben suddenly raised his left arm and tried to speak. But his whispers were too jumbled to make any sense. Again, Kat looked up to the doctor.

"He wants to tell you something. Frustrating for him. But he may have more clarity tomorrow."

"How long can I stay with him?"

"His condition will improve rapidly now he's conscious. Even so, he must maintain ample rest and sleep."

"Okay, I'll go now and come back in the morning."

As she raised herself from the chair, Ben reached for her arm. His head moved from side to side, as if pleading with her not to leave.

"There's something wrong, Doctor. The way he's straining for my arm. I sense fear in his eyes. I can't leave him like this. I can't." She pleaded.

"It maybe he's frightened he won't regain his ability to vocalise. But believe me that would be very rare in a patient who's recovering so quickly. You're welcome to stay longer. But I must stress again the importance of rest and sleep. And no excitement whatsoever."

"Okay, I'll just stay until he falls asleep."

Ten minutes later, after Ben dozed off, Kat slipped away.

As she made her way through the institutional-cream corridors to the exit, her mind turned to her job.

Can't believe our Research Centre's gone. I'd kind of like to go there ... to satisfy my curiosity. But seeing the Centre burnt to the ground might give me nightmares. All my hours of dedication left smouldering in a heap of ashes.

A throbbing head woke Kat next morning. Disturbing images of Ben's attempt to communicate had her locked in a pattern of waking and dozing with a lack of deep sleep.

There's something not right. The way he reached out for me so desperately.

In her eagerness to see him, she bounded out of bed so fast, she disturbed Juan.

"What is it, Kat?" He yawned and stretched his arms.

"Sorry, Juan. I didn't mean to wake you. I'm just so anxious to get to the hospital."

"Mind if I come along today? There's nothing much else to do now, is there?"

A jumble of wet-floor safety cones dotted the corridors as Kat and Juan dodged their way down the polished concrete passage leading to Intensive Care. When they reached reception, Elena, the duty nurse beckoned Kat over. Her face was beaming.

"Your friend's so much better this morning. He's sitting up. His wife and children are in with him now. Yes, it was a big journey for them. They reached Santiago when the flights stopped, and they were forced to come the rest of the way overland."

Kat gasped. "His wife's with him?!"

"Yes," said Elena, "his wife and two daughters. They're in with him now."

The bastard! I trusted him more than any other guy I've ever met. And he's lied to me.

"C'mon, Juan. You'd better come with me. I'm so mad, I'm scared of what I might do."

Kat stormed ahead as they made for the ward. But just before reaching his cubicle, she slowed to a crawl and tip toed up. She peered around the curtain to see the back of a blonde-haired woman sitting very cosily beside his bed holding his hand. One of his daughters seated on the other side of the bed looked her up and down.

"Hey, Grandma," she cried pointing at Kat, "Dad has a visitor."

Kat froze. The woman turned her head, smiled and jumped to her feet.

"Hello. Now you've got to be the lovely Kat. Ben was always singing your praises. And, oh … you look exactly as he described." She reached out her hand. "So pleased to meet you. I'm Sophie, Ben's mother."

Chapter Twenty-Seven

"Don't know how much your mother told you," said Juan to Ben, after his mother and daughters finally departed his bedside, "but the worlds become a very frightening place while you were in a coma."

Although his speech was a little slurred, he was making good sense. "Yes, Mom told me about the global aviation suspension. She and the girls had reached Santiago when the groundings were sprung on them. But I don't know any more than that."

"Well, when I spoke to Henri in New York yesterday, the streets had become so dangerous, he was too terrified to leave the office. He's been overnighting there because the area's being terrorised by gangs. They're mugging anyone they can, just to get enough money to buy food."

Ben shifted uneasily in his bed. "Why? There should still be enough food to go around."

"That's what happens when a population panics. The cost of food trebled overnight. And then their supermarket shelves were stripped bare. So, in retaliation, and I suppose, anger, the gangs torched the empty shops. You can't blame the poor for rioting, especially when there's nothing left to eat."

Ben suddenly slumped down on his pillow. His eyes flickered then shut tight.

"What is it?" Kat grabbed his hand. "Do you want me to call the nurse?"

He let out a moan. His head rolled from side to side. "I just had a flash from the past. The attack on me. Those men … they wanted me dead. And … those lights…"

Kat drew his hand to the comfort of her chest. "Lights? You mean … the lights you saw that night at the base?"

He gasped and fought to catch his breath.

"Quick, Juan," said Kat. "Run and get the duty nurse. He's having trouble breathing."

By the time the newly rostered duty nurse arrived, Ben had calmed. But his eyes remained closed. The nurse, who Kat hadn't met before, spoke perfect English. She checked his pulse and blood pressure.

"His readings are okay now," she assured Kat and Juan. "Was there anything that might have sparked his breathlessness?"

To me, it appeared to be a panic attack," said Juan. "He began telling us about his assault. It was as though his anxiety wouldn't let him catch his breath."

Her face scowled. "If he becomes anxious again, you must say something to deflect his troubled thinking. It's not good for him to have such upsets so soon after his recovery. I'm sure his Doctor would have explained how stress can affect a patient's breathing."

"But—"

"It's okay, Kat." Juan placed his hand on her shoulder and turned her away from the nurse. "Yes," he assured the nurse. "We will be more careful from now on."

She glared at them for a few seconds, then walked off.

"Mention of his attack came from Ben himself. We never brought it up."

"I know, I know. But …yeah… Listen, Kat, please, just let it go. I kinda got the impression his nurse was having a bad day."

On their leisurely stroll back to the hotel, Kat suggested they talk to Ben's mother and find out whether he'd mentioned his assault to her.

"Not sure about bringing that up with her. His mom appeared pretty exhausted when she left his bedside. Might be best if we leave it 'til tomorrow, Kat. At least we know her hotel's only around the corner."

Kat's pace slowed. She fell silent for a few moments. "Oh, Juan. You are right. Plus, I don't want his mother worrying, not after all she's been through."

"Hey, tell me, Kat. What did you make of him going on about … lights?"

"I assumed you knew. Ben swore strange lights lit up the sky around the base, the same night of the deaths of the Franklin team. He didn't say much at the time, but it must be playing on his mind, especially when he's still talking about what he witnessed."

As Kat and Juan arrived at the hospital next morning they spotted Ben's mother and two daughters entering the revolving front door.

"C'mon, Ben, I want to have a quick word to Sophie before we see Ben."

"Hi," Kat, puffed out, after a giddy spin through the door in an attempt to catch them up. "Hope you all had a good night."

"Oh, thank you, Kat. And so nice to have you guys with us again. Yes I'm feeling much better. Such a relief to spend a night in a decent bed."

"I have to tell you, Sophie. Just after you left Ben yesterday, he experienced some sort of flashback about his assault. Trouble is, he became so distressed, he was struggling to breathe. I've been wondering if he mentioned anything about his attack to you?"

"I'm out of my mind with worry over him. He's lost his colour, and he's so hollow-cheeked. But in answer to your question; no, he never mentioned his assault. But he did become anxious and breathless when I told him about the two strange men coming to my home the day after he left Rio to come here. They produced some sort of US military type badges—and ID, which I didn't take too much notice of—I mean, they looked so darned official. But now I'm wondering if they were who they said they were. You know, Kat, I'm fearing I made a grave mistake in telling them where Ben was headed."

Chapter Twenty-Eight

"They've named the virus the FIVe virus," Kurt announced to the team after they'd finished breakfast. "Yes the FIV is for Franklin Island Virus, and the five represents the average five-day incubation period."

The team's gloomy silence matched the overcast morning dimness enshrouding the hotel restaurant.

"Last night I took a call from The World Health Organisation. They advised there's been no documented record of this virus infecting human populations before. Not ever. It's a completely new disease. So that begs the question, where on Earth did it come from?"

Kat jumped in to break the team's silence. "That's just the point—when you said, *where on Earth*. Because I've always maintained the virus came from the meteorite crashing into the sea off Franklin Island."

"Well, okay then, go on, Kat. You can tell us more about your theory. I do have to concede you're the only survivor from the Franklin Island Station team. And you were there when the virus took hold in the emperor population."

"During my career as an ornithologist, I've witnessed some odd behaviour in birds, but believe me, nothing as weird as what I witnessed on Franklin in the days before I was rescued. To me, it appeared the birds were possessed. And then, I was forced to watch helplessly as the same behaviour gripped my team after they consumed penguin meat. And I emphasize the word helplessly. No amount of pleading with them to abandon the Station did any good. Their apathy reminded me of the way the emperors continued to sit so doggedly under the ill-fated helicopter when it attempted to land."

"Hmm," Kurt replied. "You say possessed, but possessed by what?"

Kat's premise sparked a surge of interest from the team. Soon, other questions were forthcoming; the next put to Kurt, regarding the fire at the Research Centre.

"From the call I took before I came to breakfast, it appears the fire was definitely arson. Traces of accelerant have been discovered by the forensic fire investigation team. We have to ask ourselves, why? Why would the Research Centre have been targeted just after it had been designated one of the world's leading labs for vaccine development?"

"Just adds to the spate of strange happenings," said Juan. "Look how I was targeted by a hit and run driver. And poor Ben, being beaten up and left for dead. And now we find out the Centre was deliberately set ablaze. There's definitely something sinister going on."

On their after-breakfast walk to visit Ben, Juan answered yet another call from Henri. He guided Kat into the litter strewn doorway of a boarded-up shop, should she decide she might stop and talk.

"Yes, Henri. Kat *is* with me. You're sounding a lot calmer than last time we spoke."

"I finally managed to get a cab to take me home. Took me three days to find a driver brave enough to venture out on the streets. And even then, he had a gun on his lap the whole drive there."

"That bad, eh?"

"Not sure when I'll get back to the office. But things have to settle soon. Right now, I need to speak to Kat."

Juan handed her the phone.

"Kat! I need an answer on my proposal. I think it's a very fair one. A win-win for us both."

She rolled her eyes at Juan.

"So much going on here, Henri. I'm still in shock at what's been happening. I'll sleep on it tonight. Phone me again tomorrow." She terminated the call and smiled at Juan.

"Bastard. He's only trying to save his own skin. He's so damn desperate to get Levi's job. Hah, little does he know, I intend to throw my hat in the ring too."

Kat and Juan continued their stroll through the windblown streets toward the hospital.

"We've always walked this route at night, Juan. These streets … they're so soulless in the light of day. Where are all the people? So many businesses with their doors closed."

As they approached the intensive care unit, a voice called out.

"Kat! Kat! Hello my lovely. Nice to see you again."

It was Elena, the nurse who'd been so kind when she'd first visited Ben. She came running up, her face as cheery as her greeting.

"You've come at the right time. Ben's doing so well this morning. Best I've seen him. His mother and daughters were here earlier." She checked the time. "Yes, very early. You're free to go in now."

Elena was right. The improvement in Ben was startling. There he was, propped up on a pile of pillows, his complexion rosy, and a cheeky grin on his face. And after Kat darted to his bedside and planted a firm kiss on his cheek, his grin turned to the broadest smile.

"You look so much better, Ben. Doesn't he, Juan?"

Juan nodded his agreement.

"I'm finding it easier to breathe today. That'll be why. I was panicking last time I saw you. I struggled to get enough air into my lungs."

Kat pulled up a chair. "I hear your mother, and your daughters have just been in."

"Yes, was good they came so early. I was itching to talk to Mom about those two officers who came to her door in White Plains. She's harbouring doubts about their authenticity. And I am too. I have a creepy feeling they had something to do with the attempt on my life. I reckon whoever it was who beat me to a pulp, wrote me off for dead when they ran off."

"Any idea who they were?" Juan enquired.

"It's a long story. After my memory improved last night, I recalled how, during my flight to Rio, I sat thinking about those mysterious lights outside the base. I had clear memories of how I sat on that plane trying to make sense of it all. During the flight I began to wonder if they really were choppers. Because, even with triple glazing, I'm sure I would have heard the noise. So yes, it was on that flight, I convinced myself they must have been drones with frontal white lights."

"Hmm … I guess that is a possibility," said Juan, moving in closer to the bed.

"Yeah, and I remember now; while I waited at Rio airport for my flight to Punta Arenas, I contacted the US Department of Defense and reported what I'd witnessed."

"What did you tell them?"

"I told them I suspected the lights were drones, and probably foreign. And because the Franklin team were found dead the next morning, they might have had something to do with their deaths."

"Wow!" Juan exclaimed. "And did they get back to you … for more information?"

"No. No response. Not a word. Now, don't you think that's odd?"

Chapter Twenty-Nine

"Okay, okay, Henri. Tell me what you want me to do," said Kat. *Got to get this idiot off my back once and for all.*

"But I did tell you what I need."

"Too much going on. Remind me again. What exactly do you want me to do? I know you said you want me to get you off the hook."

"Quite simple, Kat. I want you to provide a written statement confirming you were powerless to convince your team to join you when you were rescued from Franklin Station. And in that account I also want you to verify how I reprimanded you for arriving at the base on your own."

Kat heaved a loud sigh and rolled her eyes at Juan.

"You got that, Kat. Or do I have to repeat myself?"

"Okay, okay. I've got it." *Arrogant bastard.*

"Email the statement to me. Oh, and add your phone number, just in case verbal confirmation is required."

"I will. And you do the same for me: a statement proving I did not abandon my team."

"Tell me again, Kat, the reason you want it."

"Why I want it? Hah, I'll tell you why I want it. No thanks to you, Henri, I'm facing charges in Sydney of abandoning my team. I have to return to Australia sometime, and when I do, I don't want to be facing some crazy false charge."

"Right then. As I said before, it's a win-win for both of us. I'll get straight on to it."

Kat thrust the phone back into Juan's hands.

"I'll write what he wants now, and send it, in good faith. Don't know what all the urgency's about. He can't even get to his office. And I've been checking most days. Levi's position hasn't even been advertised yet."

After forwarding the requested statement for Henri, Kat bristled with restlessness. She checked the time. *Need to make my morning visit to Ben. Got to find out more about his theory on drones being responsible for the deaths of my team. None of this makes any sense. None of it.* Her musings were interrupted by an insistent request from Juan.

"Hey, Kat. Quick. Come and look at this. There's a breaking news scoop you need to see."

"What is it?"

"The FIVe virus. It's spreading like wildfire. Even surgical masks aren't stopping it. They're saying Northern California's reeling from the death toll. Now it's hitting LA and Vegas."

"But how? How could a virus transmit that quickly?"

Juan shrugged his shoulders. "Don't know, but this is beyond scary—the way it's bolting before there's been time to even begin to develop a vaccine."

"Hmm, and even more puzzling when our Research Centre was deliberately torched."

She headed for the bathroom again. "I'm going to visit Ben after my shower. Do you want to come?" She turned and paused, biting her lip. "Oh, I can't tell a lie, Juan. I'm frightened to walk there on my own, even this early in the morning."

Kat and Juan battled a raging headwind on their way to the hospital. The gusts were so ferocious, they had to hold on to each other and grab whatever solid pole or building they could cling to along the way.

"My scarf, my scarf," Kat screamed as a gust unfurled it, blowing it clean away.

"Better buy a new one," Juan strained into the wind. "Your beautiful scarf will be surfing the South Atlantic by now."

They reached the intensive care unit, panting and breathless, only to be told Ben had been transferred to the general ward. The duty nurse informed them his progress had amazed the medics.

Once again, they found him sitting up and sporting an even bigger grin. Kat pulled the privacy curtain around them, then pecked him on the cheek congratulating him on his progress.

"Hey, Ben. Do you get to listen to the news in these wards?" Juan enquired.

"No, I don't have much idea what's going on in the world. But Mom did mention the pandemic's out of control when she was here yesterday. She said the morgues are overflowing."

"Truly frightening how its spreading so rapidly." Juan took a step back from the bed. "Yeah, it'll be here before long. And no good wearing surgical masks this time round. They're not stopping the spread."

A deep frown creased Kat's face.

"Hey, Ben," chirped Juan. "Now you're out of intensive care, how about I go down to the café and grab us all a coffee?"

Ben's face lit up. "You mean a *real* coffee?" he exclaimed. "Now, that would be a treat. And can you get me a few muffins, or something sweet while you're there. Thanks, buddy."

The moment Juan left Kat alone with Ben, she wrapped her arms around him and broke into an emotional blubber. Her tears trickled into the comforting warmth of his neck.

"Oh, Ben, I can't believe what happened to you. There hasn't been a chance for us to be alone, but I have to tell you, I feel like it's all my fault."

"Why?" he asked, cradling her clammy body in his arms. "How can what happened to me be your fault?"

"You came all this way. Just for me. And that morning in the hotel room … the day you arrived. I'm so sorry. I wasn't ready for what you asked of me. I was frightened of committing. I sent you away … and—"

She pulled up a chair and sat, squeezing his hand. "Please Ben, tell me; where were you going when you were attacked?"

"I had a think about what you'd said about dating. Then I thought about our evening dinner at the hotel and how we'd be with the team. I knew that wasn't what you had in mind. So, I explored the streets for a cosy little restaurant—somewhere intimate for our very first date."

"Oh, Ben, how sweet of you."

"Yes, and it was a deserted street—where I was attacked from behind. I can't remember their faces. But you know, Kat, the weird thing is; something, and I can't quite put my finger on it, but something makes me suspect they were fellow Americans."

Chapter Thirty

"Wow, great coffee, Juan," said Ben after his first sip. "It's been a long time since I had the real thing. Would either of you like one of my cakes?" He snuck a peek in the paper bag. "Aah, I thought so. There's six in here! And they're muffins."

"No thanks, Ben," said Kat. "We know how much you love your sweet treats."

Juan grinned. "Yeah, they'll keep you happy for a while. You deserve them."

After Ben gulped down his first muffin, he sat quietly for a moment. Then, for some reason, his usual grin melted away.

"What is it, Ben? Didn't you enjoy your muffin?"

"Ah … yes, I did. Thanks, Juan. No, it's not that. My mind wandered off. You both know I've had a hell of a lot of time to sit here and brood."

"Hmm. Just like you did on your flight to Rio," said Kat. "I do remember you telling me."

"Well, since coming out of my coma, I've thought long and hard about those lights in the sky and the deaths of your team. You're both going to be shocked when I tell you my theory on what happened that night."

Kat shook her head. "With what's been going on in the world lately, I don't think anything can shock me anymore."

"Well, this will. I have to tell you, Kat. I can't help thinking your team were murdered."

"Murdered?!"

"Yes. Those puncture marks on their bodies. I'm wondering if they were made during the extraction of tissue containing the virus. I'm wondering if your team might have been targeted for the production of biological weapons. Or bioterrorism, if you like."

Kat lurched back in her chair. "What do you think, Juan?"

"I guess that would explain the puncture marks found on your team—and on the penguins. But why would the virus be on the rampage now, if it was taken for use in biological warfare? I find it hard to comprehend." He scratched his head. "To be honest, I don't know what to think anymore. I suppose the virus's development into a biowarfare agent could have been fast-tracked."

"Yes," said Kat. "And especially the fact it broke out in the US. But there again, if it was biological warfare, you'd think the bioterrorists would have needed to develop a vaccine before they released it. Would they have had sufficient time?"

"Hey, guys," Ben interrupted. "All this conjecture is doing my head in. I'd never have even considered half the points you've raised."

"You saying that," said Kat, "makes me eager to talk to Kurt and the rest of the team. I'd love to hear their thoughts."

That evening, after the team polished off their desserts, Kat stunned Kurt and her fellow colleagues by raising the premise Ben had put to her and Juan earlier in the day.

The audacious speculation of bioterrorism sparked a bout of spirited discussion among the scientifically enlightened group. But team leader Kurt's methodical summing up of the string of extraordinary events convinced the team; Ben's supposition may not be wide of the mark. Kurt also cited the conspicuous silence following the autopsies of the Franklin Station team's bodies.

"My understanding was their bodies were flown to the US for expert investigation. I've been checking every day for any press release about the examination. And I can tell you, I'm mystified as to why there hasn't been a single mention of a report from the medical examiners. It's almost as though something is being hushed up."

"So, what do you think, Kurt, regarding the fact the infection first broke out in the US? Wouldn't that also hint at it being the work of bioterrorists?"

"On the face of it, yes, it might appear that way. But the strange thing is, if that indeed was the scenario, there's been no pointing of fingers from Washington. All very puzzling to say the least."

The team stood from the table after winding up their lively discussion. They were just preparing to leave when Juan took a phone call. He covered one ear with his hand and let out a barrage of rather vocal exclamations. The team stared wide-eyed, wondering what on earth he must be hearing.

"More bad news I'm afraid," he said with a glowering frown. "I've just been talking to Doctor Ariko, from the hospital. Someone tried to kill Ben—in his hospital bed, earlier this afternoon."

"Whaat?" cried Kat.

"Yes," he panted. "Ben's mother and his daughters went down to the café to get him a coffee. When she returned she found a man wearing a balaclava in the act of choking him. In a moment of desperation, she threw hot coffee over him. But her act of bravery made him turn on her. He punched her in the head. And because of all the commotion, he took off."

Juan stopped to catch his breath. "But to make things worse, most of the hot coffee splattered over Ben's face. He's being treated now for burns and neck injuries. And his poor mother's being treated for shock, as well as tests for concussion."

Kat buried her face in her hands. "I don't believe this. When is this nightmare ever going to end?"

Chapter Thirty-One

Juan and Kat dashed out of the hotel restaurant and hotfooted it through the dark and deserted streets to the hospital. With both Ben and Sophie requiring urgent medical attention, Kat had no idea who she'd be granted permission to visit first, or even if she'd be able to see them at all. They figured it best to proceed directly to the bed Ben had occupied during their previous visit.

Kat's face lit up when Doctor Ariko sang out a cheery hello as they entered the ward.

"Is Ben still in this ward?" asked Kat, catching her breath.

"No. I take it you know about the attack?"

Kat nodded but remained silent.

"Ben's been transferred to our trauma unit for treatment of facial and neck burns. And you know his mother, Mrs Carmichael's in having tests for concussion as we speak."

"I can't believe this has happened … and in a hospital ward—" Kat's voice faltered.

"Neither can I. Our staff are in shock. From what I'm told, it was only the screams of her daughters that sent the attacker running. No better deterrent, you might say."

"This incident has to be connected to the previous assault on Ben," said Juan. "Whoever it was, or whoever *they* were, must have been *dead* set on finishing him off."

He took a sideways glance at Kat. "Oh sorry, Kat, that was a bit insensitive of me."

"No. I think you're right, Juan. It has to be something to do with him contacting the military about those lights he witnessed at the base. And even more, over his suspicions about the deaths of the Franklin team. I still think it strange he didn't receive a response to his contact."

Doctor Ariko gawked at them both in turn.

"What you're saying is news to me. What's this talk about deaths?"

Kat put forward Ben's theory on the deaths of her Antarctic team. Also, how he'd contacted the Department of Defense about his concerns upon his arrival in Rio.

The doctor shook his head. "Hey, I know nothing about how US Government departments work. But I do agree with you. Ben should have received an acknowledgement of his contact, especially when he was as closely connected as he was."

Doctor Ariko paused. His gaze turned momentarily to the corridor, then back to Juan.

"You're an American, aren't you Juan? You probably haven't caught up with this evening's news reports. How devastating the virus is right now in the US. The death rate is staggering. Mass burials every day now. Unfortunately, that's how the poor have always been buried in past pandemics."

"Any cases yet in Punta Arenas?" Kat enquired.

"Not a one. We have the global suspension on flights to thank for our good fortune. But being such a highly contagious virus, it will get here, of that I'm certain. Don't forget, we still have road transport and shipping in and out of the city."

"Oh, your eye, Sophie. The bruising. It's horrendous," Kat cried on witnessing the injury to Ben's mother.

"Yes. And run your finger over this bump under my hair," she said grabbing Kat's hand. "What an evil man. He wanted me off the scene. Same as he wanted Ben dead."

"Did you manage to get a good look at him?"

"I sure did. The chilling thing for me was, he was so well-dressed. For goodness sakes, the man could have been my next-door neighbour. My mind's all over the place right now—I feel as though I'm in a fog. I know it's not possible, but I almost thought I'd seen those eyes before—"

Doctor Ariko interrupted. "You took a severe blow to the head, Mrs Carmichael. Our testing proves you have concussion. Perhaps once your symptoms clear, you might be able to remember whether the attacker reminded you of someone you know."

After a quick supper in the hospital café, Kat, Juan, Sophie and her granddaughters were escorted to the burns unit to see Ben.

Finding Ben with his face covered in a creepy second skin-like bandage sent his mother into melt-down. She broke into tears, whimpering with regret for burning him so badly.

"Don't you go worrying, Mom," he wheezed. "I'm going to be okay." He reached out his arms for a comforting hug. "My face will heal. I'm in the best of care. Don't forget, it was your hot coffee that saved my life."

"I just want you out of this place, son … safe at home." She burst into another bout of fitful sobbing. "Oh sorry, sorry. It's just I can't see any way out. I'm terrified we're going to be stranded in this godforsaken place forever."

Tears trickled down Kat's cheeks from the sheer emotion of the moment. Sophie released her hug and turned to witness Kat's distress.

"Oh, Kat. I didn't mean to upset you. Please. Don't take my rant about getting out of this place the wrong way. Believe me, I want us all out of here. But I would never leave Ben."

Juan eased himself into the circle. "I must tell you, Mrs Carmichael. We need to demand Ben be given around-the-clock protection from now on." He patted Ben on the shoulder. "The one thing you don't want, my friend, is a repeat of this episode. I say we see Doctor Ariko before we go back to the hotel. Get some security organised for you. Either that, or I'll stay with you tonight."

"Very kind of you, Juan. And please, call me Sophie. To be honest, I had considered staying here myself. Trouble is, I don't feel comfortable about leaving the girls alone in a hotel room."

"I can understand your concern. C'mon, let's catch the doctor before he finishes his shift."

Juan was right. They just managed to catch Doctor Ariko in time to request security for Ben.

"I understand what you're saying," he replied, "but we don't have security guards in our hospital. We've never needed them. Trouble is extremely rare in this part of the world."

"Well then, can you arrange something with the local police?"

"Hey, I'm a doctor. Liaising with local police is not my role. If you want to arrange protection for Ben, you'll probably have to hire a private security guard."

"Oh, how ridiculous," Sophie ranted. "In our country a security guard would be provided by the hospital following an incident like this."

"Listen, I can sympathise with you. However, Punta Arenas is not the United States. Now, if you'll excuse me, I have my wife and children waiting for me out in the car park."

As the doctor bounded off, Kat called him out. "Is it me, or did we just witness a different side to Doctor Ariko?"

Chapter Thirty-Two

The next morning at the team's hotel breakfast, Kurt happened to mention he'd seen the World Ornithological Society inviting expressions of interest for the position of president.

Kat jerked back in her chair. She nudged Juan's knee and whispered in his ear.

"No wonder Henri kept pestering me for his statement. Yes, and the bastard still hasn't reciprocated with what I asked him for. Hah, now I know why."

"Shush." Juan tapped Kat on the arm and whispered, "I'm trying to listen."

Kurt told the team he assumed, Henri, being Vice President, would no doubt win the position.

Kat couldn't help herself. "But he's not even an ornithologist," she piped. "Henri's background's in finance. Now doesn't that say something about how far removed from reality large organisations become when they expand?"

"Oh," said Kurt squirming in his chair. He gazed around the table. "That's news to me. Well in that case, what was the man doing studying penguins in Antarctica?"

"He didn't study *any* penguins. His role was simply to accompany Levi Stanton. Nothing more than a Society funded junket. But as you all know, Levi only made it as far as Christchurch."

Kurt picked up on Kat's animosity toward Henri. In a shrewd move, he changed the subject, enquiring about the progress of Ben and his mother.

After their return to the hotel room, Juan voiced his concern at Kat's agitated state.

"You're all worked up over the Ornithological Society vacancy aren't you, Kat? You're so damn twitchy."

"No! It's not the vacancy. I told you at breakfast, Juan! It's about Henri lying to me. He promised me a favourable statement in exchange for the one I composed for him. And he hasn't damn well delivered."

"Do you want me to make a call for you? You can hit him with a timely reminder."

"But I hate talking to Henri. The guy makes my skin crawl."

"At least you'll get it off your chest. You're going to give yourself a heart attack carrying on like this."

"Oh…" She screwed up her face. "The bastard's got me right where he wants me. Out of contention."

Juan shrugged his shoulders. "It's up to you, Kat. I guess I could speak on your behalf. Tell him you let me in on the full story. Yeah, that might swing it for you. I can put the guilts on him."

Kat stood, wringing her hands, shifting from one foot to another. She exhaled hard. "I don't know. I really don't know what to do. Doesn't seem fair dragging you into my bitch with Henri."

"I'm not feeling *dragged* in, Kat. I'm doing it for you. You've been my friend here. You're always here for me."

Kat stared at him, dumbstruck at the emotion in his voice. She tensed, struggling to resist the seductive attraction of his eyes. "Oh, go on then. It's not as though he doesn't know you, is it?"

Juan proceeded with the call. "He should be up by now. There's only an hour difference in our time zones."

"Henri? Henri? Oh …" Juan paused and scratched the back of his head.

"Really…? I see. I didn't realise things were so bad there. Can't you call an ambulance?"

Kat began wriggling with impatience.

"Sorry, I don't know what else to suggest," said Juan. "Well, you take care, and I'll call back later in the day. Check how things are going for you guys."

"What in the hell was that all about? Fobbing you off with some bullshit drama by the sound of it."

"No. I spoke to Henri's neighbour. An elderly woman called Marie. She found him lying on the floor in the apartment lobby this morning."

Kat gulped in shock.

"Yes, she said he's in a confused state. He's in a bad way, Kat. Hasn't eaten for some days. She says they're all too frightened to leave the building, or even open the front door—the virus, the riots, and the gangs."

Kat flitted her eyes around the room, as if struggling to find the right words.

"I don't much like Henri, but I'd never wish anything unkind on him. I heard you mention an ambulance."

"Marie says they'd be waiting days for an ambulance. Every hospital in the city's overflowing. Sounds as though the entire place has gone to hell."

"Too many people crowded into one place. Never dreamed I'd be saying this, Juan, but maybe Chile is the best place to be right now. We're probably a lot safer way down here in Punta Arenas than in most other cities in the world."

He nodded his agreement and chuckled. "You're right. And here you were, so worked up about The Society appointment going to Henri. Hah, the way things are looking, Kat, he won't be in any state to apply for president of the World Ornithological Society."

Chapter Thirty-Three

Juan sat bolt upright in his hotel bed, spooked by the sound of plaintive whimpering.

"Kat? Kat? Are you okay?" he called out in the darkness.

The bleating continued. He leapt to his feet and raced to Kat's bedside.

"Kat. Tell me. What's happened?"

"I … I just had the worst dream," she blubbered, raising herself from her pillow.

He sat down on the bed. "Do you want the light on—to bring you back to reality?"

"No."

His hand reached out in the darkness to the clamminess of her body.

"Hey, you're wet, and you're shaking. Are you feverish at all?"

"No, nothing like that. Just a bad dream. About Henri. Must have been today's dreadful news."

"Let me give you a hug—ground you to where you are right now. My mother used to soothe my childhood nightmares with long hugs."

Her trembling body melted into his embrace.

"It's okay. It's okay. You're safe now." His breath huffed warm on her neck.

A sudden need for comfort overpowered her. She clung to him with a needy fervour. He commenced a gentle rocking, as a parent would to comfort a frightened child. But then his lips began nuzzling at her neck. The feel of unwanted kisses panicked her. Suddenly, the image of Ben's handsome face eclipsed the nightmare about Henri.

Juan. What's he trying to do? "Juan! This is *my* bed! Pleeease! Get off me. I'm okay now."

"Sorry, sorry, Kat. I didn't mean to…"

"Just go back to your own bed," she snapped. "Forget my bad dream ever happened."

Getting back to sleep proved impossible for Kat. Her mind kept churning. Over and over and over. Her harrowing night—the horror of her nightmare—and even worse, Juan's attempt to take advantage of her in her most vulnerable moment.

I really thought Juan was my friend. Now I've lost my trust in him. I'm not sharing this hotel room with a man I don't trust. No. I want him out. Either that, or I go. But then, why should I? Where would I go? And what might Ben think if I move out of here?

With her mind disturbed, Kat crawled to the edge of the bed, with the intention of taking a warm shower. She perched for a moment, cocking an ear toward Juan's side of the room. The deep rhythm of his breathing reassured her he'd fallen back to sleep. Fumbling in the dark, she found her robe and inched her way to the bathroom door. After turning on the light, she clicked the door to lock. Then she double checked to be sure.

Kat savoured the soothing flow of the water on her skin, luxuriating in its consoling warmth, washing away the turmoil of the night.

The first subtle light of dawn was already creeping in when Kat emerged from the bathroom. She stopped in her tracks. There was Juan, up and dressed and seated on the sofa. He jumped up the instant she appeared.

"Hey, Kat. I want to apologise for last night."

Kat flew at him. "I'm not willing to place myself in that situation ever again. Either you go, or I go!"

He looked away.

"Hell, Kat. I'm sorry. I know … I'm a man, and that's what got in the way of our friendship last night."

"And how much of that sort of bullshit do you think I was forced to endure from the guys at Franklin Station? You crossed a line last night, Juan. Yes, and even worse, you have the cheek to call Ben *your friend*. Yet, you would have betrayed him," she snapped her fingers, "just like that. No, Juan. I'm not on Franklin now. I don't have to put up with any more blokeish crap."

"Okay, okay." He raised his palm and diverted his eyes to the floor. "I'll take my shower, then I'll go and ask reception if they have any spare rooms."

Just as he promised, after his morning shower, Juan skulked from the room and approached reception to enquire about a possible reservation. His heart sank on hearing all the rooms were currently reserved. But the receptionist asked him to wait while he conducted a thorough check.

After a few moments, the young man returned to the desk, his forehead already bearing the crease of having a hectic day.

"I was right, sir. There are no suites left in the hotel. However, the manager informed me, we do have one room temporarily unoccupied. How about I ask our guest if you might occupy his room until he returns."

"Great," said Juan.

"And you're one of the research team staying here, aren't you?"

Juan shot him a quizzical look and nodded.

"Would it be presumptuous of me to ask if your sharing situation isn't working out—just to give our customer a reason for wanting the room so urgently."

Juan dipped his head.

"Leave it with me, sir. I'll get straight on to it for you."

Later in the morning, Kat made her usual visit to Ben's bedside. On her way to the ward, she ran into Sophie and her two granddaughters.

"Morning, Sophie," she cried as she breezed through the corridor. "And how's my favourite patient doing this morning?"

Sophie grabbed her hand. "Our boy's not so good today, Kat. He had a restless night. The nurse tells me he's battling an infection. Definitely not his usual self—a bit down in the dumps. As you know, that's not like our Ben."

Kat cupped her hands over Sophie's. "Oh no. Feeling down is the last thing Ben needs after all he's been through."

"He also complained about a member of your research team wanting his hotel room until he's discharged from hospital. He appears mystified as to why. Tell me, it's not you wanting his room is it Kat?"

"Ah…" She gulped. "No. No, it's not me."

"Well then, I'll leave you to talk to him about what's going on in your team. Hopefully you can ease his concerns."

Chapter Thirty-Four

With her heart pounding, Kat headed straight for Ben's bedside. The usual glint in his eyes was missing. His head drooped. A sadness dulled his face.

"Kat," he said with a plea in his voice. "Why didn't you come to me first about my hotel room? I thought you and I could talk about anything."

Kat closed her eyes and shook her head, wondering just what he was implying.

"Why wouldn't I want you to share my room," he pleaded. "I would have been over the moon about us being together at last. But why … why go to the hotel about it before talking to me? I feel like … well, like I've been bypassed." He paused in thought. "Can't you comprehend how it feels for me?"

Kat gulped. She had to think on her feet. *Do I tell him it's Juan wanting his room, or do I tell him it's me? Shit!*

At that moment, Juan walked in.

"Hi, Ben." He paused for a moment. "I suppose Kat's told you about what happened last night?"

Ben raised himself on his pillows giving Kat a blank stare.

"She obviously hasn't," said Juan. "I'm feeling pretty awful, Ben. I want to come clean, because I regard you as a friend."

Juan related how Kat's horrific nightmare had her whimpering in distress. And how he'd raced over to her bed to comfort her.

"Yes, I comforted her like my mother comforted me when I suffered my childhood nightmares—you know; rocked her in my arms. But I guess I got a bit … you know, caught up in the moment and my lips grazed her neck. Then Kat got angry. And quite rightly so. That wasn't what she needed. I'm sorry."

He stood for a moment, teetering.

"I came to tell you, Ben, because I don't want to lose your friendship."

Kat reached for Ben's hand. "I was the one who asked Juan to move out to another hotel room. I had no idea it would be your room."

Ben chuckled. "And here was I thinking you'd finally accepted my marriage proposal—well, amongst other things."

Thanks for your honesty, Juan. Must have been hard for you coming here and telling me something so awkward."

Juan lowered his head.

"Okay," said Ben. "Let's just forget it. Carry on as friends." He let out another chuckle. "So now I'll have a temporary roommate when I'm discharged."

Kat flew to the bed and kissed Ben on the lips.

"Oh, Ben. I've never known a man like you. You're *the* most understanding guy I've ever met."

Ben grabbed her hand. "So does being understanding make me marriage material then?"

She looked down. "Mmm. I'll talk to you about that later."

"Alone at last," said Ben, after Juan left the ward.

"I know. You've been getting so many visitors."

Kat dragged her chair in closer then paused for a moment. "So … are you sure you're good with Juan, after what happened?"

"Yeah, yeah. He came across as being totally open and honest."

"You might think I made a big deal about last night, but for me, the abuse I suffered on Franklin Island still haunts me. Their behaviour was the pits. I was forced to endure unwanted leering and lewd remarks from the young guys at the Station. You'd think I'd be hardened to it by now, but I never did get used to it. And what happened last night, in the sanctuary of my own bedroom—well, it brought it all back."

Ben squeezed her hand. "You should never have had to put up with being hit on in your workplace. And I agree; to be subjected to behaviour like that in your room would have been the last straw. But I do admire Juan for his honesty. And because he was so open, I'm willing to forget what happened and remain friends. But my question to you is, can *you* let go of it?"

Kat shuffled in her chair. "Ahh…okay then. You're right. I'll let it pass."

He beamed his usual wide grin. "Hey, you still haven't answered the question I posed earlier—about me being marriage material."

"Of course you're marriage material! I'll marry you as soon as you're discharged. Plus, I wouldn't want to miss the opportunity of having your mum and the girls here for our big day."

He reached out his arms to her and they luxuriated in a long embrace.

"I'm so happy at how well you and Mom get along. Not that I ever had any doubts you would."

"She's so like you, Ben; easy going and good fun. I realise it's going to take longer to get to know Chloe and Zara, but I'm sure I will, in time."

"They're at *that* age Kat, if you know what I mean."

She looked him in the eye. "I do know what you mean. Anyway, it's the best thing we could both wish for; your family being here for our wedding."

"Yes, and I doubt they'll be going home in a hurry either. Not with the doom and gloom of this morning's news. You won't have seen today's headlines—about the devastation the virus is wreaking on the planet. And you being an ornithologist, Kat; there's disastrous news about the world's penguin population." He pointed to the floor. "A copy of the front page is on the bottom shelf of the dresser there. Doctor Ariko prints himself an English speaking copy every morning then passes it on to me. Take a look."

She reached down into the dim depths of the lower shelf of the bedside dresser and gagged at the mustiness. *Hmm, smells as though the cleaner's been forgetting to dust down here.*

Ben flinched at her gasp as she registered the apocalyptic headline.

WORLD'S BIGGEST EXTINCTION EVENT SINCE THE DINOSAURS

Scientists lament the demise of our planet's entire penguin species.

Scientists today concluded, there is little doubt the once abundant penguin, native only to the Southern Hemisphere, is now extinct. The rapid transmission of the fatal Antarctic virus far eclipses any ecological disaster humanity has ever known.

Kat cupped her hand over her mouth. "Whaaat?! I don't believe what I'm reading. They're saying there's no penguins left. Every bird has succumbed—completely wiped out. Oh, Ben," she cried, "we really are living a nightmare."

Chapter Thirty-Five

Kat arrived back at the hotel to find Juan busy sorting his belongings. He looked up but didn't utter a word.

Oh, no. I was hoping he'd be gone by now. She eyed the door, thinking it might be prudent to leave him to his packing and head to the café for morning tea. But just as she turned to go, he called her back.

"Hey, Kat. My apologies. I've been held up with moving out. I phoned to check on how Henri is. Remember? I promised I'd contact his neighbour, to see how he's doing."

"What's happening then?"

"She said they finally managed to get some food delivered. But at an incredible cost." He let out a laugh. "Apparently, the delivery guy wore a plastic bucket over his head when he came to their door. Two slits for his eyes. Marie said she screamed; the guy spooked her out big time. She told me people there are taking the most bizarre precautions—plastic bags, even DIY frames with cling wrap around their heads. Sounds as though no one's trusting masks anymore."

"I'd heard masks weren't providing protection. Anyway, I take it Henri's okay now?"

"I had a quick word with him. His voice was feeble. He's desperate to escape New York City, but he can't see any way out."

Not long after Juan left the hotel room, there was a knock at Kat's door. It was Sophie, her face ghosted white in contrast to the flashy red of her tightly zipped puffer jacket. She met Kat's stare, then darted her eyes away.

"Sophie. Are you okay? It's not Ben, is it?"

"No… No, Ben's fine. It's just … Kat, we have to talk. Ben asked me to come and see you. I know you're making plans to tie the knot as soon as he's out of hospital—and that isn't far away now. But there's something Ben hasn't told you—something he should have discussed. It's too painful for him to divulge right now."

Kat flinched as a myriad of uncertainties whizzed through her brain. They seated themselves around the coffee table and Sophie began telling Kat about the break-up of Ben's marriage and the ensuing tragedy.

"You see, with Ben's career, flying helicopters all over the world, he had little choice but to allow his ex-wife custody of his girls. And unfortunately, Veronique … who I'm sorry to say, has always been emotionally unstable, jumped headfirst into another relationship. This new man moved straight in with her and the girls. I wasn't happy because the guy had a drug dependency. And emotional health problems to boot. That's how they met—at their therapy sessions."

Kat shuffled in her seat.

"Oh, Kat, I'm so sorry." She wiped away a tear. "I gather Ben hasn't told you *any* of this, has he?"

"No, he hasn't. I had no idea."

"I'm afraid Veronique became a victim of domestic violence from the moment this new man moved in. Even worse, the girls witnessed his brutality on many occasions—way too many occasions. Anyway, it all came to a horrific and violent ending. In a moment of self-defence, she shot the man dead. I have no doubt he would have ended up killing her if she hadn't put a bullet in him. But the dreadful thing was, the girls were in the house when it happened. Nothing will ever take away from the horror they witnessed that day. They're so damaged, Kat. If they weren't here visiting their father, they'd still be attending their scheduled counselling sessions."

Kat lurched her head back on the sofa, lost for words.

"I can tell what I've revealed has come as a shock to you. And please, please, don't blame Ben for not telling you. I'm sure if he hadn't suffered the attack, he would have had the fortitude to sit down and disclose the whole horrendous tale."

"So, Ben and Veronique … they *are* divorced?"

"Oh yes, that was easy."

"Where's Veronique now?"

"She's serving time. But because of the horrendous abuse she suffered, she'll soon be out of prison."

At the evening hotel dinner, Kurt spooked the team with alarming news about the rapid progression of the FIVe virus. From what he ascertained from the day's news reports, as the infection stormed its way south through the US, a clear pattern began to emerge. This virus was exacting a far more lethal toll on Caucasians than any other race. The discovery was also said to explain why there'd been minimal infiltration over the border into Latin America.

"This latest finding," he informed the team, "has spawned an explosion of conspiracy theories. The leading premise being, the virus was somehow pirated on its emergence, then hurriedly engineered by enemies of the West."

Kat gasped. "Hey, that scenario would explain the deaths of my Franklin team. Remember those puncture marks on their heads? And what about those strange lights at the base the night they died? Ooh, I can't wait to tell Ben."

On her way to re-visit Ben in the evening, Kat mulled over the bombshell revelations Sophie had disclosed earlier in the day. Those disclosures left her with a muddle of disturbing questions, and her mind reeling with dark doubts.

How honest is Ben, that he failed to tell me such crucial details about his past life? Will Veronique demand custody of the girls after she leaves prison? And how will Ben cope if he loses custody? And if the girls do stay with Ben and me, how is their emotionally scarred state going to affect our marriage?

Chapter Thirty-Six

Ben's very first glance said it all. Kat stood back from his bedside allowing him time to calm.

"Mom's told you hasn't she?" His voice grated with emotion.

"Yes, Ben. She has told me." Kat dragged her feet toward his bed and stood in silence.

"I'm sorry, Kat. I didn't get to tell you myself. The right time just never came … there was always someone else here. Either that, or I wasn't feeling well enough."

Kat's brain whirled with recall. *Yes. Maybe what he say is true. Perhaps the right moment really hasn't come up for him. And after all, he has renewed my trust in men.*

She pulled up a chair close to his bedside. "Listen, Ben. I understand the right moment not coming up. I know there's always been nurses buzzing around. And you've had a constant stream of visitors." She sat back in her chair trying to figure what to say.

"I have to tell you this, Ben. There's a heap of questions in my mind about our future together. Your mother tells me your ex-wife will be out of prison soon. Have you ever considered she might attempt to gain custody of the girls?"

"That's one big headache hanging over me all the time. But given what happened in the past, and what she exposed the girls to, I can't imagine the court allowing her a second chance at custody."

"You haven't told me much about your marriage, or what went wrong. If we're going to be together, I deserve to know. After all, I did fill you in on what happened with my fiancée."

Ben puffed out a resigned sigh. "It was my work. I was always off—somewhere—around the globe. Veronique was forever complaining about me not being there for her and the girls. But she did marry me knowing piloting choppers is my life—my forever career. And she didn't say no to all the money and the good life my job provided."

"Hmm," Kat mused. "So … after our wedding, and the pandemic, you'll be off again travelling the world. Hah," she laughed, "and I'll probably be doing the same. Does that mean your mother will continue her grandparenting duties?"

"Yes, but only while you and I are away. Don't know about you, Kat, but I do get long stints at home as well."

"I'm sure Sophie will appreciate me having the girls when I'm home."

"Hello, Ben." A voice called out from behind the curtain. It was Doctor Ariko. They both baulked at the sight of his mask and face shield. "Oh … how are you, Kat?" He hesitated for a few seconds. "I'm afraid I have some worrisome news. We all knew this was inevitable. And Ben, I had hoped you would have been discharged by now."

"What's happened, Doc?" Ben enquired.

"The hospital's just admitted a number of FIVe virus victims. They're in a bad way. Arrived this morning on a cargo vessel. Thing is, it's our duty, as medical professionals, to treat them—futile as that may be."

Ben and Kat eyed each other, too numbed to speak.

"All I ask is, please don't panic. These men are in quarantine. I assure you, you're quite safe," he said as he strode off.

"Quite safe? Bloody hell, how safe is *quite* safe?" Kat exclaimed after Doctor Ariko departed the cubicle. "Alright for him to say that, with his layers of protective gear. Although I did hear masks don't provide protection from this virus—not from the news reports coming in."

"But he did emphasise we shouldn't panic."

"What? About a virus that wiped out the global penguin population. It could do the same to humans. Anyway, why can't they let you go home, Ben? You seem fit and healthy to me."

He shrugged. "Seems my pain still needs to be managed. That's what the nurses tell me."

"Well, I don't feel safe being in here anymore. Why should you?"

"What are you saying?"

"Why can't I manage your pain for you, at home? If pain relief's all they're keeping you in for. This virus is way too contagious to guarantee anyone's safety. C'mon, let's go—get you out of this place."

"But I've only been up to the toilet and for showering. I don't think I'd make it to the end of the ward, let alone walk to the hotel."

"I'll find you a wheelchair. There's got to be one somewhere."

Kat sprang to her feet and raced away.

Just as she promised, Kat returned to Ben's bedside after a few minutes pushing a hospital wheelchair.

"This doesn't feel right, Kat, just up and leaving."

"Listen, Ben. It's taken me all my life to find a man like you. I'm not going to lose you to some ghastly disease."

A cheeky grin washed over his crumpled face.

"C'mon then, legs out first." She turned the wheelchair around in readiness.

He wriggled over to the side of the bed and slid his legs out from under the covers. His breathing quickened. Even this minimal movement proved an effort. She let him rest a moment. After catching his breath, he raised his body and sat himself on the edge of the bed, feet dangling to the floor.

"I'm not sure we can do this, Kat. I'm a pretty hefty guy. Usually there's two sturdy nurses to help me out of bed."

She reached out. "I'll take your weight until you get seated in the chair. C'mon, quickly now, before we get sprung."

He grabbed her outstretched arms the same way a frightened child might seize hold of a parent in deep water. He then launched himself toward her with one emboldened heave.

"Aargh," Kat shrieked as her legs folded beneath her. Ben's sheer weight felled her to the floor. She lay, pinned by his bulk and screaming in agony.

Kat's spine-chilling cries alerted the duty nurse something was terribly wrong. She burst into the cubicle and froze in horror at the tortuous tangle of bodies beside the bed. In a few moments, a team of staff commenced a delicate rescue operation. Lifting Ben back onto his bed was a difficult, but manageable manoeuvre. However, Kat's excruciating pain and her screams, made for a complicated rescue. The team administered powerful painkillers and gently eased her onto a stretcher. Ben's face paled to white as she was wheeled off to Emergency.

First medic on the scene in Emergency was Doctor Ariko. Although he'd been advised of the accident Kat had suffered, he was anxious to know exactly what caused her trauma.

"Oooh," she moaned. "I felt sorry for Ben—being confined to his room for so long, I wanted to treat him to a visit to the cafe."

"Hmm," the doctor mumbled from behind his mask and visor. "Not a good idea. From what the team tell me, you have tingling sensations. We can't rule out a spinal cord injury. I'm about to send you for a series of scans. And hey, never mind worrying about Ben being stuck in here for so long. You may well be looking at being a long-term patient yourself."

Chapter Thirty-Seven

Lingering in her lonely cubicle, waiting for the results of her scans proved a frustrating experience for Kat. She'd never once been a patient in a hospital. Despite her attempts to remain positive, she twitched with anxiety. All she wanted was a progress report—anything to relieve her ruminating on her dire situation. Her stomach churned every time she contemplated never being able to walk again. *I can't live out the rest of my life in a wheelchair. I can't! I'd sooner be dead.*

Then came the recriminations. Her ill-conceived idea to spirit Ben away from the danger of the FIVe virus. *Damn it. Now, I've ended up exposing myself to the very same danger.*

The sound of a familiar voice lightened the dark clouds of hopelessness. It was Kurt. But she jumped at the creepiness of the protective visor shielding his face.

"Apologies, Kat. I'm not taking any chances—not now the virus is here in the building."

"I know, I know. I don't blame you, Kurt. It's just … the shock of seeing you decked out like a spaceman."

"I couldn't believe it when I found out what happened to you. You're going to be okay, I take it?"

"I don't know yet. I've just had a scanning session in that whirring dishwasher thing. Now I'm playing the waiting game."

"Mind if I sit down?"

"Please. Pull up a chair. Oh … I'm so relieved to have some company. Tell me, have you been to visit Ben?"

"No. I did venture into the ward, but the nurse said his wife and children were with him. I might visit him on my way out."

"His wife," cried Kat. "No, Kurt. That'll be Sophie, his mother. But, hey, she would take that as a compliment."

"I swear the nurse said the woman was his wife."

"She must have been confused as well. Tell me, Kurt. What's going on out there in the big wide world? You're always so on top of the latest news."

He reached under his visor and stroked his yellow-grey beard. "Hmm, some rather sensational theories on the virus are spilling out thick and fast. Especially the rumours about it being engineered to kill Caucasians. There's even an allegation of CIA involvement. And that scenario is said to have been leaked by an insider. The informer says it's a deliberate strategy to reduce the global population."

"Whaat? But why pick on Caucasians?"

"Hah. It might be a lot of hot air. It may simply be, because Caucasians were first infected, the infection latched on to them and became more easily transmissible to that race. Who knows."

"Has there been any more speculation about who removed the tissue samples from my team?"

"There's been nothing more on that one. But don't forget, although there were no records of those shoeprint impressions being manufactured anywhere in the world, they were human sized, so probably not alien beings as some have speculated."

"Still weird though."

"To be honest, Kat, all I want, and I'm sure all you want now, is to return to our families and wait out the nightmare."

"Me too. Oh, to look out on a sparkling Sydney harbour from my window seat as I'm flying in. How many times have I stared out and never appreciated what I—"

Kat's nostalgic outpouring was interrupted by Doctor Ariko. A definite twinkle shone out from behind his visor.

"Hello," he said with a cheery inflection, before introducing himself to Kurt.

Kat explained how she and Kurt had first met.

"I have some rather remarkable news for you, Kat. Your scans are all clear. Amazing really, considering how you presented when you arrived in Emergency. But there again, shock and trauma can sometimes mimic other symptoms. You'll be pleased to know I'm giving you the all-clear."

"You mean … I can … leave?"

"Yes. I'll get the duty nurse to do a couple of quick observations, then you're free to go."

"I'm well enough now to visit Ben," said Kat, as they dodged the bustle of the hospital's hectic emergency ward. "Won't he be surprised to see me? Are you coming, Kurt?"

He agreed. They made their way through the maze of bland creamy-coloured corridors to Ben's ward.

"Who's she?" said Kat as she peered toward Ben's cubicle at the far end of the ward.

The curtains had been drawn right back to reveal a huddle of visitors surrounding his bed.

"That'll be his wife. Remember the nurse told me his wife was visiting."

Something bombed the pit of Kat's stomach. She slowed her pace.

"Kat!" Ben cried out. "You're here. You're okay. What a relief."

"Yes. I've been discharged." She glanced at the strange woman, then looked to the frozen statue who was Sophie.

"Kat, this is my ex-wife Veronique. She was so desperate to be with our girls, she drove for days. Can you believe it? She drove here all the way from New York!"

Kat threw her a curt nod. Why in the hell is he praising her?

Ben then went on to reaffirm his plans to marry Kat on his discharge from hospital. Veronique cast her a daggered once-over. Top to toe.

Scrawny bitch. Giving me the evil eye. I'm out of here.

"Sorry, Ben. I have to go. I only had a minute. Doctor Ariko wants to see me so he can work out a date for my follow-up check. Bye, Sophie. Bye, girls. And I'll see you at dinner tonight, Kurt."

Chapter Thirty-Eight

Next morning, Kat jolted awake from a vivid dream. As she reached into the darkness for the light switch, the jubilant expression on Ben's face played in her brain. *Oh, yes. In my dream he was dancing. Dancing! With a woman I don't know.*

The heartbreaking image was enough to fire her insecurity. She ran to the bathroom and jumped in the shower. Her hands flew into overdrive: squeezing out the shampoo, pouring out the liquid soap, upping the water pressure.

I've got to see him before that bitch of an ex turns up.

The decision came easy. Kat skipped breakfast and rushed out the hotel door for the hospital. The freezing late winter wind snatched at her breath as she set a cracking pace through the deserted streets and past the depressing rows of boarded-up shops.

The curtains around Ben's bed were tied right back when Kat entered the ward.

Great! He's on his own. I've got him all to myself for once.

As she drew closer, she saw he was sitting up. A strange sight. He was wearing a set of headphones, his eyes glued to a small-screened television set suspended above his bed. She walked right up and waved her hand to catch his attention. He jumped and wrenched off the headphones.

"Kat! You're so early. Everything okay?"

"Just wanted us to be on our own for once. Anything wrong with that?"

He shuffled back on the pillows. "No. No, of course not."

"I didn't know they had TVs available in here. How did you come to get one?"

"Yes, they have a special rail above each bed to attach a hired set. But you can only have it on if you wear headphones."

"So how come you've just found out about it then?"

"Ahh … Veronique made enquiries. She arranged the hire for me."

A burst of heat percolated Kat's body.

"Ooh, Veronique *arranged* it for me," she mocked in an affected voice. "So … what else has Veronique *arranged* for you?"

"Nothing." He shook his head. "No … nothing else."

"Are you sure you two *are* legally divorced?"

"Sure, we are. But ours was an amicable parting. We made an agreement to remain friends—for the emotional wellbeing of the girls."

Ben's semi-permanent smile usually charmed Kat. But she tensed at the grin on his face whenever he talked about Veronique. *He has no idea what it does to me when he keeps talking about her.*

Ben jumped at the chance to explain how having a TV meant he now had access to news about home, and in his own language.

"I've just been watching the mammoth excavators they're using to dig mass burial sites around the outskirts of New York. So much beautiful parkland being dug up. Hundreds being buried at a time. It's heart wrenching, Kat. And the worst thing is, I have no idea if my old schoolmates and workmates, or even my friends and neighbours are still alive."

The glint of sorrow in his eyes was enough to shake Kat from her cynical mindset.

"I'm so angry about what's happening, Ben. But I don't know who to direct my anger towards. If this virus has been spread deliberately, what sort of scum are behind it? So evil—if they've plotted the world's worst ever epidemic."

"I have to tell you, Kat. Because none of us really know how much time we've got left, I've made up my mind. We're getting married. Married, tomorrow."

Kats face creased with confusion. "Tomorrow? What do you mean, tomorrow?"

"I've arranged for a celebrant to be here at ten o'clock in the morning. Are you good to go?"

Kat gaped. "I … I … yes, yes, of course I'm good to go. It's just such a … well such a shock."

"It's taken a killer pandemic to tell me life's too short. It'll just be you and me. A brief, private ceremony."

"But, your mother? And Chloe and Zara?"

"I've discussed it with them. They're all fine with the arrangements. They know that's what we want, and they respect our wishes. But I have promised them a formal ceremony when we all get back to White Plains."

He wriggled and reached under the pillow. "Remember this? It's the ring I showed you when I first asked you to marry me." His face beamed. "At least you can say you were engaged for a day."

She leaned over him, kissed his lips, then slid the ring on her finger.

"Just a tiny bit loose. But we'll get it resized. Don't want to lose it now, do I? More importantly, I don't ever want to lose you."

She squeezed his hand.

"You know, Ben." She purred. "I never thought I'd live see this day again; engaged to be married. I've carried the burden of not being able to trust a man for way too long."

Her hand waved, flashing the dazzling diamonds in the light. "But look at me now."

After a few minutes of precious time alone together, the duty nurse slipped in to check on Ben. Despite her poor command of English, he had come to comprehend most of what she said, especially when she snuck him extra helpings of sweet treats.

"News bad this morning, Benjamin," she said from behind her visor. "Lost last sea man from ship this morning. All four passed now, in last twenty-four hours. We all very sad."

Kat and Ben gazed at each other, struck dumb by their proximity to such horror.

"But some goodness news, Benjamin," she added. "No one else catch virus in ho-pital."

"Thank you, Rosa. So terribly sad. Where were the four men from?"

"All four from Canadians. But rest of them not catch. They from here.

Rosa surveyed the flashing monitors then moved on to attend her next patient.

"Because those Canadian men were off a foreign owned ship, it's more than likely they were the only Caucasians onboard," said Ben after Rosa left. "The very target group the virus appears to have been engineered to kill."

Kat buried her face in her hands. "Oh, Ben, I want out of this nightmare. I was on such a high until she hit us with that news. What's happened to the beautiful world we used to know?"

Ben drooped his head. He didn't answer.

"Tell me Ben. Do you think all this might be the work of aliens?"

"But why would aliens bother to target just one ethnic race?"

Chapter Thirty-Nine

Oh, what to wear, what to wear. Kat's head spun with the excitement of her wedding day after leaving Ben's hospital bedside. *Tomorrow's going to be the most memorable day of my life.*

A new beginning— for us both.

After arriving back in her room, Kat opened her wardrobe, looking for her most elegant attire for the big day. The clothes she'd purchased locally were limited, but she did have one very smart ivory coloured business suit she'd had consigned from her favourite boutique in Sydney. An ensemble purchased with one very significant career interview in mind. Even better, this suit had never been worn, either at work, or in Punta Arenas. In a flurry of vivacity, she slipped into the outfit and paraded in front of the mirror, hands racing over the jacket, smoothing out the lay of the cloth. *Oh yes. This is the one.* Her jubilant face beamed back at her from the mirror.

After a solid workout at the gym, Kat joined Kurt, Juan, and the team for their evening dinner. She deliberately flashed her engagement ring under the luxuriant lighting of the table's low hanging chandelier. Despite her repeated gazes at the ring's dazzle, no one at the table said a thing. Nor did they pick up on her bubbly demeanour.

Men! They're all the same. Only interested in what concerns them. Well, damn them, I'm not going to state the obvious.

Flopping her hand down into her lap under the table, she turned her attention to the conversation. Her ears pricked up when Juan used the word *crippled* to describe his homeland.

"I've been meaning to ask you, Juan," she interjected, "have you heard anymore from Henri?"

"He's not answering my calls. And neither is his neighbour. I have grave fears for them. I'm wondering whether they've succumbed—either to starvation, or to the virus. I don't know what to think."

"Any word about Henri from Society headquarters?"

"Nothing. Headquarters reception just keeps ringing out. It scares me to even think what might have happened. As I said before, the country's crippled. Everything's at a standstill. Canada, even the UK, all paralysed. It's as though there's been a deliberately planned attack on the West."

"I've come to the same conclusion," said the ever-well informed Kurt, drawing downward strokes on his shaggy beard.

After hearing such disturbing news, Kat would normally have gone to bed with a fast-beating heart, trying desperately to turn off and get some sleep. But tonight, her head luxuriated in the excitement of tomorrow's ceremony and her deep affection for Ben. Her brain began savouring all his delightful quirks. How he rubbed his tummy when hunger pressed, how his eyes lit up whenever he contemplated the sweet desserts on a menu. And cutest of all, his semi-permanent grin. Sleep came quickly. A deep contented slumber. The kind of slumber she'd been yearning for most of her life.

For once, the alarm woke Kat on her wedding morning. Usually, she'd be stirring well before the jarring beep zapped her ears. A quick stretch, and she was up and ready to embrace the day ahead. Breakfast this morning, as arranged, would be delivered to her room.

After lingering in the hottest of showers, she let reception know she was ready for her first meal of the day: a skimpy serving of yoghurt and mixed berries, which took on the appearance of a mere crumb on the huge breakfast trolley.

Now, my beautiful outfit. Once again, she smiled at the smartly tailored cut the suit projected in the mirror. Her whole face lit up as she admired the flattering elegance the outfit flaunted. After a final check at the bathroom vanity, she raced to the door. But as she reached for the safety chain, her hand fell to her side.

"Ben did say 10 o'clock. Or was it 11 o'clock?" She gazed around the room trying to jog her memory. *Too much going on.* She paused for thought and exhaled. *I don't care, I'm too excited to sit it out in a hotel room for one more minute.*

This time, as Kat entered the ward, the curtains shrouded the cubicle around Ben's bed. She checked the time. *Almost ten. Maybe I did get the time wrong.*

She approached and peeped in through a gap to make sure she wasn't disturbing the duty nurse. She recoiled at the sight of Ben wearing a mask. His closed eyes and slumped shoulders alerted her something wasn't right.

"Are you okay, Ben?" she whispered grazing her hand over his.

He jumped at her touch. His eyes fluttered open.

"No… Not okay." He hesitated, shook his head, then commenced a pitiful snivelling.

"I've just been told Veronique's come down with the FIVe virus."

"Whaat? Oh no."

He averted his eyes. "She's in the isolation ward now. They're trying to treat her. But… well, you know what happens… She's going to die, Kat, Veronique's going to die." His face contorted with anguish as he broke into a blubber.

"Oh, Ben, Ben, I'm so sorry. But what about Chloe and Zara? And what about your mother? And … you? When was she last in here?"

"It's okay, none of us have any symptoms."

Kat turned away. No symptoms? Hmm, not yet.

"The celebrant I booked will be here any minute now. But I'm sorry, Kat, I don't think I can go through with the ceremony today. Are you okay if we postpone?"

Now why did I know this was coming? That damn woman. She's still ruling his life.

Chapter Forty

Just seconds after Ben floored Kat with talk of postponing their wedding ceremony, a chirpy greeting from behind interrupted her despondent mood. A friendly face greeted Kat as she turned around.

"You must be our celebrant," she said to the petite cherub-faced woman.

"Hello, lovely people. No, I not your celebrant. I Marcia, your translator."

"Translator?"

"Yes, celebrant will perform ceremony in Spanish. English-speaking celebrant got cold today. She make last-minute rearrange. But is good for me. I get job today!"

Kat threw Ben a pleading expression.

"Oh, Ben, we can't let two people down. This beautiful lady has given up her time, and the celebrant will be here any minute now."

Ben shook his head. "I can't, Kat. Not today, of all days."

"It's *her* again, isn't it?" she moaned. "It's *always* about *her*. Well, I'm sorry, but my clock's ticking too, Ben." She slipped the engagement ring from her finger and threw it on the bed. "I've had it with you and your damn ex." Her fists clenched at her side. "For me it's now or never. If I walk out of here, you won't see me again. And don't think I'm just saying it."

The translator's mouth gaped open. She didn't know where to look.

The sound of approaching footsteps relieved the tension. The celebrant raced in, puffing and blowing. She greeted Kat and Ben with a nod, then addressed them in Spanish.

"I sorry for being late," translated Marcia. "You ready to start ceremony?"

Ben removed his mask, picked the ring up from the blanket and gestured to Kat to hold out her hand. He slipped the ring back on her finger. "Okay. Yes, we're ready," he said, his face tortured with emotion.

Kat raised her brow in confusion. There was nothing more to say.

Smiles broke through tears for both Kat and Ben as they exchanged vows. Then a tender impassioned kiss swept away the earlier tension. She beheld his forever laughing eyes, her head spinning.

I need to tell my wonderful man my deepest darkest secrets: how much I've longed for this day. How very old I felt before he came into my life. And how I'd given up all hope of ever finding someone to spend the rest of my life with. I need to share my hopes and fears with him if I want the honesty I crave in our marriage. No. I won't forget this moment. From now on, I'll strive to bare my innermost self.

"I'm sorry, Kat," said Ben, after the celebrant and translator left the cubicle. "Sorry for how I discounted your feelings."

"Oh, Ben. And didn't I do exactly the same?"

"But we made it, Kat. We're together now. That's all that matters."

"And we've both learned something—about each other. How about a *real* kiss for the bride now we're on our own?"

Word soon circulated about the couple who'd taken their marriage vows behind closed curtains in Ben's ward. The nursing staff quicky collaborated to make the occasion even more special. The judder of a clattering trolley and a party of giggling staff broke the usual solemnity of the hospital.

"Surprise, surprise! Congratulations, Mr and Mrs Carmichael." A full chorus of voices rang out.

To Kat and Ben's amazement, a cart festooned with dainty assorted cakes, and urns of hot tea and coffee came wheeling in. Heading the celebration party were Doctor Ariko, and Rosa.

"I had a word with the office," said the doctor. "They told me this is the first ever wedding service to be performed in our hospital. So, we did a quick rally around to make it special."

For almost half an hour, the staff came and went, mingling around the bed, sipping their drinks and nibbling on the assortment of exquisite cakes.

The sombre silence of the ward returned to haunt Kat and Ben following the cheer Doctor Ariko and the nursing staff had presented.

"So quiet, Ben."

"I know. Feels almost spooky now."

"Just one thing about today that's puzzling me," said Kat with a serious tone. "How did you choose my wedding ring?"

"That was easy. Mom brought me a catalogue from one of the local jewellery shops. I chose it for you myself."

It was almost lunchtime for Ben, so Kat made up her mind to return to the hotel to shower and change into more comfortable attire. She promised to make her usual afternoon visit later in the day.

As she entered the hotel, Kat spied Juan and Kurt, gripped in a standing conversation in the lobby. She made a discreet approach and stood behind Juan.

"Kat! You're looking rather formal today in your suit," said Kurt.

"I am. And for good reason." She giggled and flashed her rings. "Ben and I just got married. A private ceremony. Just the two of us. Oh, and the celebrant."

"Great news, Kat!" Kurt replied.

"Oh … well. There you go," Juan added. His reaction was somewhat muted. But Kat had him worked out.

"Care to join us for a quick bite and a celebration coffee in the café?"

"Thanks, Kurt, I will. But yes, it will have to be quick. I'm dying to kick off these ridiculous heels and hit the gym."

Over a brief lunch, Kurt divulged yet another scoop of disturbing news. His face grimaced and he drew a breath.

"Such a worrying newsbreak this morning, Kat." He tugged his beard. "There are even more unconfirmed reports that a CIA insider leaked details of a scandal about the FIVe virus. It's an anonymous disclosure and claims the virus was masterminded as a tool for depopulation."

"So, intentional corruption of the virus no longer just a rumour," said Juan.

"If the leak is true, it explains a lot—about the weird happenings after I left the Station. The shoeprints for one. And those puncture marks on my team's bodies."

"Well yes, the shoe prints have always been a mystery. You know, I've often wondered whether those intruders might have had one-off shoe soles specially made up and bonded to their shoes."

"Oh Kurt, I would never have even thought of that. You should have been a detective, or … or maybe a crime writer."

"Clever, yes," he replied. "But the sheer genius has all the hallmarks of an intelligence spy agency."

"But it's still all conjecture," said Juan, discounting Kurt's well-measured suggestion.

The thunderous stare on Kat's face had him backpedalling.

"But … I suppose it's not entirely inconceivable—"

"Anyway," Kurt interrupted. "The reaction to the leak has led to rioting. Who can blame them. Almost every American has lost a friend or loved one. Even more suspicious; they haven't come up with a vaccine. Right now, the White House is surrounded by hordes of angry protestors. They're estimated to be in their thousands. The ringleaders are inciting them to storm the building. They're promising the American people the White House will be trashed and looted, then burnt to the ground."

Chapter Forty-One

Kat walked in to find Ben struggling to pull off his headphones.

"Ben, you're just like Kurt—you've become a bit of a news freak, haven't you?"

He darted his eyes away from the screen. "Hmm, what troubled times we're living in. I'm watching yet another re-run of our president begging the threatening mobs not to storm the White House. And when I say the man's begging—the poor guy's almost on his knees. He's just given his word to the people, declaring the virus was never engineered as a means of de-population."

"And you believe him?"

"Maybe. But…"

"I still say the pathogen was taken from my dead team members. And I've been saying all along it came from the Antarctic meteorite and then jumped the species from penguins to humans."

"That's looking more and more the likely scenario, Kat, especially when you were the only one who didn't consume penguin meat."

"I just bumped into Kurt at the hotel. He brought me up to date with all the drama—you know—about the reaction to a possible CIA insider leak. He's saying the reason Americans are seething with anger, is that almost everyone has lost someone they know to the virus."

"He's not wrong there."

"Oh, and I must tell you, Kurt told me his theory about the strange shoe prints found at Franklin Station. He said the shoe soles were one-off custom-made prints; reckons they were glued on over every day branded shoes."

Ben gasped. "Wow. Whoever would have thought?"

"It's looking now as though Kurt was one step ahead in his thinking. But you should have heard Juan's scepticism. The guy thinks he's so damn smart."

Ben moved his mouth to reply but froze.

"What's wrong?"

He heaved out a moan. "Oh, Kat. It was you mentioning Juan. I just remembered. I had a … well, I'm not sure exactly. But a couple of nights ago I had, like a bad dream, or … I don't know, maybe it was a flashback. It was about Juan. He was trying to kill me. Suffocate me right here in my bed. Was just like a replay of my attack."

"Juan?! Oh, Ben, where in the hell would that have come from?"

"As I said before, I don't know. I … I really don't know."

"Excuse me, Ben." An imploring voice hurtled him back to the present. Doctor Ariko edged in. And this time he wasn't laughing or nibbling on cakes. A mask and visor put an end to his earlier exuberance.

"I'm afraid I have some very grave news, Ben." He pulled up a chair close to the bed.

"I'm sorry to inform you, your ex-wife, Veronique: she passed away less than an hour ago. Please accept our sincerest condolences. Believe me, our team did everything possible to try to save her, but this virus is like nothing we've ever witnessed. Unbelievably deadly."

Kat let out a whimper. The doctor backed away as she raced to Ben's side.

"Ben, Ben. I'm so sorry. I really am." She swaddled him in a comforting hug.

Between sobs of grief, he sputtered out an emotional cry. "It's starting to happen here, Kat. Can you believe it? It's happening here. Now someone *we* know has been lost to this freaking virus. Where's it all going to end?"

Although Doctor Ariko withdrew, he hovered at the cubicle entrance. This time, waiting his moment to impart positive news. Once Kat sat back down on the bedside chair he moved in and addressed Ben. The news the doctor delivered was the timely boost Ben had been waiting for. A date had finally been set for his discharge from hospital. A firm promise he'd be out in less than a week.

After Doctor Ariko's departure, Ben bared all on the rollercoaster ride of events of the day.

"I still can't believe what's happened today, Kat," he said shaking his head. "Veronique passing on the same day I remarry."

"I know. So very tragic."

Kat gulped. *I feel so rotten now about my jealousy. And the horrible way I spoke about her.*

"Please forgive me for the way I talked about Veronique. That was my own insecurities boiling over. Those same old feelings of inadequacy are always there, simmering below the surface."

"But why?" He gazed into her eyes. "Why would a beautiful soul like you ever consider yourself inadequate, Kat?"

She shrugged. "I never feel good enough. Never. And I never have felt good enough. Sometimes I think that's why I was cheated on all those years ago. Almost as though I deserved it—like I wasn't worthy enough." She paused and looked to the floor. "Listen Ben, I know it's been devastating for you losing Veronique. Especially today of all days. But maybe now we need to think of our future. Remember how we planned our formal wedding with all your friends and family in White Plains? We have our dream life to look forward to. Our day is going to be so special."

The rattle of the afternoon tea wagon put a halt to the conversation. The routine had become all too familiar to Ben. While *he* was more than happy with the bland hospital coffee, Kat always headed down to the café and brought back a barista-made coffee to enjoy with him.

With a hot coffee in her hand, and making her way back into Ben's ward, Kat baulked at the ruckus coming from the end of the ward. As she drew closer, the familiar bawl of Ben's earlier grief again tortured her ears. *How odd. I wonder what's set him off again?*

She halted at the entrance to his cubicle to see the doctor seated at his bedside.

"Ben! Are you okay?" she asked, rushing toward him.

His face flushed red. He couldn't answer for choking on a barrage of sobbing tears.

Doctor Ariko stood to his feet. His face glum behind his visor.

"More sad news I'm afraid," he whispered. "Ben's mother, Sophie, and his two daughters have just been admitted with symptoms of the virus."

Chapter Forty-Two

The news of Veronique's passing traumatised Ben. But when told his mother, and daughters, Chloe and Zara, had come down with FIVe virus symptoms, he plummeted to a state of emotional numbness. After an outburst of blubbering, he couldn't bring himself to speak. Kat sat caressing his hands, allowing him time to absorb the gravity of the situation. Although summoning every ounce of comfort she was able to muster, a nightmare of menacing thoughts raged through her head.

My survival, Ben's survival! Our lives are at risk now too. If we stay here we're both going to die. We've got to get away.

Kat mulled over her dilemma.

Ben's frozen with the fear of losing his family. What will he say if I suggest we save our lives by fleeing? But if Sophie and the girls should die, how will I ever live with myself after taking him away from the ones he loves? And if I leave him alone, he's going to think I abandoned him in his hour of greatest need.

She chewed her lip. *It's all too much. I can't see any way out. We're all doomed to succumb to this freaking virus.*

Time at Ben's bedside dragged for Kat. Her anxiety maxed out, leaving her a fidgeting mess. When Doctor Ariko made an unexpected return, garbed in his gown and visor, she reminded him of how pointless the wearing of protective gear had been proven to be.

"You're right. There's several well-researched studies concluding this infection can't be checked by masks. But our Director insists we continue to use them." His gown lifted as he shrugged. "If I want to hold on to my career, I'm duty-bound to follow her mandate."

Kat shook her head in disbelief.

"Tell me, Kat," he whispered from behind his visor, "is Ben coping okay now? I'm wondering whether a sedative might be in order, especially if he's continuing to display symptoms of emotional shock."

"I'm so worried about him, Doctor. I've noticed his breathing going into irregular spasms—almost as though he can't catch his breath."

"Ooh… Okay. I'd better get the duty nurse to perform some checks."

Kat heaved a sigh as he raced off. *Don't tell me there's going to be another delay with his discharge.*

She gazed at Ben. Her heart sank at the lines of anguish etched on his face. Once again, she took his hand in hers and gulped before offering words of comfort, all the while knowing, they might not be true.

"Oh, Ben, my gorgeous husband, don't worry, I'm here for you. Everything's going to be alright."

Kat stayed close, her stomach whirling with butterflies as the duty nurse ran a thorough check of Ben's vital signs. When she finally completed her task, Kat asked how he was. The nurse smiled and gestured a cursory thumbs up. In broken English, she apologised, inferring only Doctor Ariko can divulge medical results.

A long and stony silence ensued as Kat sat waiting for the doctor's return. She slouched back in her chair, resigned to her inability to comfort Ben. Her only hope was the promised medication would be the fix he needed to subdue him.

Kat possessed little awareness her all-consuming concern for Ben masked her own distress at Sophie, Chloe and Zara, succumbing to symptoms of the virus.

As she waited for the doctor, flashbacks from her past haunted her head. The heartache of losing family wasn't new to Kat. As an only child in her teens, she suffered the agony of losing both parents in just under two years. At a vulnerable age, she endured hour upon distressing hour, comforting them in hospitals and hospices, fully aware their conditions were terminal. But right now, with her focus channelled exclusively on Ben, the anguish of the past remained just that. In the past.

The longer Kat sat at Ben's bedside ruminating over the death of Veronique, and the infection besetting Ben's family, the more she tortured herself over leaving Franklin Island Station without her team.

What if Henri was right? Maybe I was negligent in abandoning my team. Staying on with them at the station might have been enough to prevent the curse ravaging the whole of humanity.

Kat was thrown from her ruminating by the whoosh of Doctor Ariko's long blue gown sweeping into Ben's cubicle.

"I have good news for you, Ben," he panted. "All your test results are favourable. I've prescribed a medication to get you back to feeling your old self. And best news of all," he turned to include Kat, "I'm very confident you'll be discharged tomorrow morning. But I do have to tell you, I'm only approving this earlier discharge as a preventive measure. I most certainly don't want you coming down with the virus."

Ben roused blubbering. "No! No! How can I leave my mom and children in this place, all alone to die?"

His face rumpled and his jaw tremored with emotion.

"Ben, Ben, please listen to the doctor," Kat consoled him. Her eyes darted to Doctor Ariko.

"Listen, Ben," said the doctor. "Even if you were to remain in hospital, you would not be permitted to have any contact with your family. The chances of infection are horrifying."

"You mean … I might never see my mother … my children, again?"

"Believe me, we're doing everything possible to save them. And let me assure you, compared to your ex-wife, they're all in far superior health than she was when she fell ill. So please, don't jump to any conclusions about not seeing them again."

Ben drew such a hard breath his cheeks bulged, and his face turned red.

"Hey, hear me out, Ben," Doctor Ariko snapped. "For your own survival, and for the survival of your beautiful new wife, I want you discharged ASAP."

"No! I'm not leaving. You can't make me. I'm not going anywhere!"

Chapter Forty-Three

Doctor Ariko had little choice but to concede to the demands of Ben's impassioned protest. He wouldn't permit him to visit his infected mother and daughters, but he made a snap decision to allow him one more night's hospital stay, knowing the prescribed medication would kick in and ease his distress.

Kat flustered with apprehension about leaving him in such a troubled state. But her day had been tumultuous. All she craved was a tough work-out in the gym and a decent night's sleep.

After settling back into her hotel room, Kat flopped onto the sanctuary of her bed and slept for close to two hours. She moaned at the head-spinning grogginess bearing down as she struggled to wake. As hard as she tried, she couldn't summon the energy to move. Resigned to her exhaustion, she lay—a medley of thoughts buzzing through her brain.

Surely Ben will be well enough to leave hospital tomorrow morning. I don't want him staying there any longer than he needs. That place is full of the virus. But what if he's already been infected? Such strange things he's coming out with—like Juan trying to suffocate him.

The longer Kat contemplated Ben's allegation, the more unfounded suspicions rattled her head.

How did Juan come to be in the Antarctic team anyway? And why was he so quick to discount Kurt's theory on the shoeprints? I've never felt one hundred percent comfortable with him. Hmm, I wonder if he had anything to do with the fire that destroyed the Research Centre?

Kat readied herself for a late night. Her plan was to get Kurt on his own after dinner and instigate some subtle digging on her suspicions about Juan.

The team enjoyed yet another evening under the elegantly jewelled chandeliers of the hotel dining room, with its over-attentive waiting staff and five-star cuisine. Kat satisfied her appetite with a petite vegetarian ricotta tortellini entree. No main. No dessert.

Over the course of the evening, she was careful not to stare at Juan. Yet she cast a watchful eye over his every interaction.

Could he be? She asked herself. *Yes, he might very well be ... the spy, who'd leaked so much about our team. The scumbag behind the sabotaging of our wonderful Research Centre.*

Kat's determination to have a one-on-one with Kurt, kept her in full spark all night. She voiced her opinion in every conversation, her hands flying with animated fervour.

After dinner, Kurt spoke of his unease at the latest news reports from the United Kingdom and Europe. He told the team the virus had stormed into these nations like a raging wildfire; the population reeling under its deathly onslaught. The media likening the devastating infectiousness of the FIVe virus and absence of preventive medication, to the infamous black death that decimated Europe all those centuries ago.

Kats eyes goggled as she posed a chilling scenario to Kurt.

"Do you think we're all facing the same death sentence as the penguin species—the total annihilation of mankind, just like every single penguin has been wiped from the planet?"

A hair-raising silence hung in the air. Kurt tugged the end of his beard.

"The mass extinction of the penguin species was freakish, to say the least. Their disappearance has dumbfounded the scientific world. A disaster of this proportion has never happened—well not in recorded history. The last mass extinction was sixty million years ago, and if my memory serves me well, that disaster was caused by an asteroid." He paused and looked to the ceiling. "Ah … or was it sixty-six million years ago? Sorry, I can't remember which it was."

"But Kurt, do you think it might happen to us—the extinction of all humanity?"

He gazed around the table. "As you're all aware, we Caucasians have no immunity to the FIVe virus whatsoever. Other races are faring better. But don't forget viruses have a nasty habit of mutating. And that's what the medical world fear most."

"Hey!" Juan exclaimed. "All this doom and gloom's making me depressed. Plus, I'm pretty tired. Think I'll say goodnight."

Kat effected a silent hand clap under the table. *Yaaaay! And goodnight to you. I couldn't have asked for better timing. Now, how do I get Kurt on his own?*

Juan's mention of fatigue prompted a mood change in the team. One by one they excused themselves. Kat was quick to pounce on Kurt.

"Would you have a few moments to spare, Kurt? I need to talk to you about Ben."

He checked his watch. "Of course. Do you want to stay here or move to the lounge?"

After choosing the privacy of the lounge, Kat began by relating the emotional trauma Ben was suffering.

"Ben was more cut up than I imagined he'd be over losing Veronique. I mean … well, they were divorced."

"I never met his first wife, but I suppose they would have been through a lot together after raising two daughters."

"Are you aware, his mother, Sophie, and both Chloe and Zara, have all come down with symptoms of the virus?"

"What!? No!"

"I'm afraid so. Ben's an emotional wreck. I want him out of that disease-ridden hospital. But he's refusing to go—wants to stay near them. He's crazy. I'm so frightened, Kurt. I'm scared I'm going to lose him."

"Hmm, some dilemma for the poor fellow. But I guess you have to respect his wishes. And I'm sure he's well aware of the risks."

There's something else concerning me. How much do you know about Juan?"

"Juan?"

"Yes. I know he's a graduate in ornithology, but I was wondering if any background checks were carried out when he joined the research team? Do you know where he was employed before he came to the Antarctic Base?"

"You know as well as I do, Kat, that's highly confidential information. Anyway," he glared over his glasses, "why are you asking?"

"Ben tells me he had some sort of flashback. Or … maybe it was a dream, about Juan trying to suffocate him in his hospital bed."

Kurt sat quietly for a moment. He rubbed his chin, contemplating the assertion he'd just heard.

"Hmm, that sounds like some sort of hallucination. I hate to tell you this, but if I didn't know better, I'd swear Ben's already succumbed to the first stage of infection with the virus."

Chapter Forty-Four

Kat tossed and turned all night. Her mind raced as she battled to process the unfolding tumult of her day.

No, I don't believe what Kurt said. Ben does not have the virus. She kicked off the heavy covers and turned over for the umpteenth time. *But what if we are all going to die? Can't Ben and I at least spend our last few days on this earth together? We've had no time to ourselves; time we deserve as a newly married couple.*

Kat wanted to boost her staying power by joining the team for a nutritious breakfast. She walked into the restaurant and faltered in her steps. A table of furrowed faces stopped her in her tracks. The team's usual friendly greeting was muted. Kurt caught her eye.

"Sorry, Kat. We're used to you skipping the odd breakfast, but this morning, Juan's not turned up. We're all worried. He never, and I mean never, misses his breakfast."

"Oh," said Kat pulling out her chair and taking a seat.

"Just to be sure," said Kurt, "I've sent one of the hotel staff to check he's not fallen ill."

She pursed her lips. *Hmm, I wonder if he's figured our suspicions about him. He's probably cut and run.*

For once, Kat ordered a breakfast every bit as hearty as those of the other team members. She wasn't about to let rumours about Juan compromise her day.

Just after the breakfast orders were taken, the hotel manager approached Kurt and whispered in his ear. Kurt sprang from the table and followed the man. She gazed at the startled faces of her colleagues. *Something serious must have happened. Bet I'm right. Juan's vacated his room. He's done a runner.*

No, I'm not going to let Juan spoil my day. Kat began munching her granola the moment it arrived. An eerie silence continued until Kurt's return. His stance was stooped and his face grey.

"I'm afraid I have distressing news about Juan." He stood, wavering. Appears he's been the victim of foul play. The hotel manager found him deceased in his room."

Cries of disbelief rang out from the table. Kat threw her hand over her mouth. Such shocking news wasn't what she'd expected.

"Nooo! Oh, Kurt, this can't be true," she blubbered. She sat in tearful silence for a moment, reflecting on what might have happened. "But, that night … when someone tried to run him down on our walk to the hospital. I thought then, how fortunate he was to have survived."

"Of course, I'd forgotten all about the attempt on his life. That incident may well be related. But why? What's behind it?"

What else can possibly go wrong today? Kat drew a deep breath as she entered Ben's ward. To her surprise Ben sat seated in a chair beside his bed, flashing one of his huge grins.

"I've been cleared to go, Kat. Got my pills." He rattled the bag in front of her face. "Let's get out of here."

Kat baulked at the startling change in his mood. *Why isn't he insisting on staying for his family? Have the meds they've prescribed numbed his grip on reality?*

Although she'd been yearning for this moment, she couldn't come to terms with the abrupt change in his disposition. A flutter of guilt churned her stomach. *I'm taking him from his mother and daughters, and he doesn't even register.*

"Ben," she leaned down and kissed him. "So good to have you back to your old self. Hope you're as ready as I am for our honeymoon getaway."

They were interrupted by the swish of a fully garbed and visored nurse entering the cubicle. Kat beckoned her away to ask about Ben's discharge.

"Are you sure Ben's ready to leave?" she whispered.

"Yes, he ready," she replied in broken English.

"What about the virus? I thought Doctor Ariko was worried he might fall ill."

"No. He all okay. He go now. But you help him his medication."

"But his change in mood? He's gone completely opposite."

The nurse placed an arm around Kat's waist and escorted her back toward the cubicle. She pointed to the bag of medication, smiled, then walked away.

"Come on, my gorgeous husband, we'll go back to the hotel and pack our bags. One night in our room, then we'll leave in the morning."

On their ride back to the hotel, Kat informed Ben of the news about Juan. He remained uncommunicative and straight-faced. She queried him about the flashback he'd experienced, where he claimed Juan had tried to suffocate him. She gawked at his unexpected reply.

"No, that wasn't a flash back, Kat," he replied. "It was a bad dream." He paused for a moment, his fingers twitching at the button on his jacket. "I need to come clean and tell you what sparked the dream. I've been burning with jealousy ever since I found Juan sharing a room with you when I first arrived here."

As they entered the hotel lobby, Kat spied Kurt locked in deep conversation with a group of local police officers.

"Can we sit here for a while, Ben," she said, leading him to a plush gold embroidered loveseat. "I need to ask Kurt a few details about our travel to the coast tomorrow."

After a lengthy and patient wait, Kat sprang to catch Kurt the minute the officers departed.

"Kurt, Kurt," she cried as he began heading back to his room.

"Ben's just been discharged." She pointed toward him, seated in the lobby. "We were hoping to leave tomorrow for the coast—remember you said we were welcome to honeymoon in the bird observation quarters."

"Course you can. Hang on." He fumbled for his wallet. "I'll give you the door combination number. Here—the number's on this card. Don't, whatever you do, please don't lose it. And you'll need to top up the pantry. But there is general store, just a short walk away."

"Yes, I recall us all ogling at your pic of the historic wooden store."

She hesitated for a moment. *I have to ask him.*

"Any more details about Juan?"

"The police think the gunman used a silencer. Juan must have unknowingly opened his door. His body was lying just inside, so they think the perpetrator never even entered his room. I also reminded them of the previous attempt on his life."

Kat winced. "Oh, poor Juan. But why? Why…?"

"That's where it gets interesting, Kat. One of the detectives who combed the room found concealed papers linking Juan to some sort of counter-bioterrorism organisation. It appears our dear friend Juan, was some sort of crusader—an activist if you like, working on the side to outfox rogue nations developing contagions for evil intentions."

Kat gulped. Her eyes moistened. *Oh no. How could I have been so wrong about poor Juan?*

Chapter Forty-Five

On the evening of Ben's discharge, dinner took on the presentation of a rather special event. Knowing how much he loved his food, and the deprivations of bland hospital fare, Kurt organised the best ever foodie's welcome home for Ben. The celebration commenced with a selection of gourmet nibbles and a huge chocolate mud cake. Ben beamed out his trademark grin as he rubbed his stomach.

"Thank you so much, Kurt," Kat enthused. "You're so kind, organising all this for us."

She also appreciated how such a fun evening would keep Ben's mind from the tragedy afflicting his family.

Once again, I've been proved wrong. Kurt's so caring. Still can't believe how judgemental I was the first time I met him. Hmm, and then there's my misjudgement of Juan! This has been a personal wake-up call for me. I'm sure going to remember how wrong I was... One of life's lessons.

As always, after most of their hotel dinners, the late evening coffee time allowed Kurt the opportunity to update the team with the latest news on the virus and its global impact. But first, he presented his personal overview of the findings relating to Juan.

"Because the documents found in Juan's room link him to a counter bioterrorist organisation, I think we can be almost certain the footprints at Franklin Station were the work of some rogue nation."

"I don't know about you guys," Kat interjected, "but it's now become pretty obvious the virus was extracted from my team for bioterrorism purposes."

Everyone nodded their agreement.

"Yes," said Kurt, "and my guess is they're the same crazies who firebombed our research centre. They, whoever they are, had inside information our centre was the first place the virus was being assessed for the development of a vaccine."

"Something's still bugging me, Kurt," Kat interrupted. "Where do you think the virus came from in the first place?"

"That, my dear Kat, is the biggest mystery of all."

"Well, I still believe it arrived on the meteorite that crashed into the sea off Franklin Island. I mean—just look at the timing."

"Nothing's off the table, Kat."

"The other thing puzzling me is why a vaccine hasn't been developed somewhere else."

"I wondered the same. But scientists are classifying this virus as having a similar genus to a rhino virus—the one that lumbered us with the common cold. Don't forget a vaccine has never been produced for that respiratory illness."

"Has there been any change to the survival rate?" Another of the team enquired.

"Last I heard, the mortality rate was still sitting at around ninety-six percent. But the other tragedy is the toll on emotional health. There's been a staggering upsurge in the number of suicides. So many people are not coping."

A shiver raced through Kat's body as Kurt delivered yet another doomsday update on the global fallout from the virus.

"In some places in Europe, they've run out of able-bodied men and women to help bury the dead."

An avalanche of chilling images flashed through Kat's brain. Visions of rotting bodies heaped in the streets. Dead bodies being tossed like garbage onto trucks.

She'd first become aware of the ravages of the Great Plague on a visit to a London Museum. Those mournful cries of 'bring out your dead' blurting from the interactive headphones, came rushing back. Now it was happening here. Right here, at the very bottom of the world, in far-flung Punta Arenas. A torrent of menacing questions haunted her mind.

Is this the final apocalypse humanity's always dreaded? How much time do Ben, and I have left?

Ben's long sleepy yawns prompted Kat to check the time. The late hour, and his recovering physical and emotional state alerted her it was his bedtime. She gripped his hand extra tight as he stumbled his way from the restaurant, past the newly stationed security guards, and up to their hotel room. Clearly, the medication was taking a physical toll, but logic told her he'd end up in an emotional mess if it was discontinued. And if he succumbed to a downhill spiral, the romantic getaway she so eagerly desired would not eventuate.

With fatigue sapping his energy, she helped Ben undress. A strange clammy sweat percolated from his skin as she manoeuvred him into bed. After making him comfortable she made a mad rush to the bathroom. The muffled sounds of gagging echoed through the tiled bathroom as Kat purged the chocolate mud cake she'd pigged out on earlier in the evening.

Why do I keep doing this to myself? I felt so uptight at dinner, I got carried away again, bingeing on food I'd normally avoid.

After a swishing gargle with mouthwash, she crept out and crawled in beside Ben. His breathing laboured hard. Deep and rhythmic. He'd already fallen into a sound sleep. She lay for a few moments, disappointment clouding her mind. She reached out, aching to feel the allure of his body. But she stopped short, her hand laying impotent on the cold sheet. Tears welled in her eyes.

This is not the thrilling moment a bride yearns for on her first night with her new husband.

Chapter Forty-Six

The acrid taste of vomit fouling her mouth woke Kat from her slumber. She scrunched up her face in disgust. A hazy recall of last night's purge of the chocolate mud cake drifted into her mind. She clenched her fists. *Why the hell did I binge on that?!*

But her self-loathing morphed to bliss as she reached for the comfort of Ben's body.

"Kat, you're awake. I've been wondering … wondering whether to get up and take a shower."

"We don't need to rush. Let's enjoy our first morning together." She took a swig from her bedside glass of water then edged in closer, wrapping her arm around him and squeezing him tight. But she cringed at the clammy dampness moistening her palms.

"Are you feeling okay, Ben? You feel red hot."

"I am kind of sweaty. And my head hurts. Do you mind if I go take a shower?"

I'd love to tell him I'll join him. But…

"Go on then. Help you cool down."

She heaved a sigh as he perched on the edge of the bed rubbing his eyes.

Hmm, think I've married me a big huggy teddy bear. Looks as though a quick cuddle's all I'm going to get on our first morning together.

"What are we doing today, Kat? I've forgotten."

"We're off on our honeymoon. Remember? Kurt's given us permission to stay at a beautiful bird observation cabin on the coast."

He turned his head, his face contorted. "But … Mom … and… No! I can't leave my Mom. I can't leave my girls."

Oh, here we go. I forgot to give him his meds last night.

"Listen. They're getting the best possible treatment, Ben. And don't forget, visitors are not permitted. Not even family."

"You're not hearing me! I want to stay close. The coast's too far away."

"But Ben, it's our honeymoon." She rolled her head away, concealing her welling tears.

After Ben closed the bathroom door, Kat crept up and waited for the hiss of the shower. She then phoned room service and ordered Ben the menu's finest: the full english breakfast.

Ben can't resist a good feast. I'll insist he takes his meds before eating. His drugs will calm him right down. Time out on the coast is the distraction we both need.

By the time Ben emerged from his shower and shave, breakfast had just been delivered. Although covered with a gleaming food dome, the sizzling aroma of crispy bacon permeated the room. His eyes lit up. Kat removed the plate cover then rattled his medication containers.

"These first, thank you. Doctor Ariko's orders. Remember?"

She dispensed the pills and handed him a glass of juice. He glugged the tablets down then grabbed the plate of bacon and eggs.

As Kat sat sipping her herbal tea and munching on her slice of wholemeal toast, a dull ache began coursing through her forehead. She squirmed at the lather of perspiration dampening her flushed skin.

Oh no. I had a feeling I wouldn't escape. Looks like we're both succumbing to the virus. Five days incubation period. Hmm.

She began counting backwards trying to remember where she was, or who she was with five days ago. But it was all too hard. She straightened her posture with a rush of resolve. *Well, if we are going to die, I'd sooner we were surrounded by the beauty of nature. I don't want to spend the final days of my life locked up in some soul-destroying hospital cubicle.*

After breakfast and a hurried shower, Kat paced the hotel room, itching to hit the road. She'd planned ahead and packed their bag the previous day. Now came the waiting game.

How long's it going to take for the medication to kick in and calm his distress?

"C'mon Ben, let's go and treat ourselves. How about morning tea in the hotel café? Their homemade cakes are scrumptious."

Despite his supersize breakfast, Ben sprang to his feet, raring to go.

"Oh wait," she cried, remembering they might both be infected with the virus. "No, I'll have the coffee and cakes delivered to the room."

When the waitress knocked, Kat opened the tiniest crack in the doorway and stood well back. She requested the trolley be left outside saying she'd wheel it in herself.

While Ben gorged himself on cake, Kat sat sipping on her coffee, her stomach churning with apprehension. *Are his meds going to kick in? Is he going to agree to leave for the coast?*

After two hours of constantly checking the time, Kat threw caution to the wind and ordered a taxi to the hotel's front portico.

"Time to leave for our honeymoon, Ben. We've been talking about our getaway for so long now. Today's the day. Our taxi will be waiting downstairs."

He shot her a blank stare. "You mean, we're going on vacation?"

"Yes. We both need a break away."

He nodded, picked up the bag and followed, like a well-disciplined schoolboy.

The lift doors opened to a smile from the lobby security guard. Kat heaved a sigh of relief. So far there'd been no more mention of his mother or his daughters.

Kat smarted at the cold air smacking her face as they stepped outside. The shapely spiralled topiaries lining the hotel portico rocked to and fro in the blustery wind. The only glimmer breaking the gloomy grey morning was the dazzling yellow taxi pulling up.

"Huh, and Kurt promised me, spring's the sunniest time of year in Punta Arenas," she grumbled out loud as the driver opened the rear doors.

"Sorry love, weather here's much the same as where I come from," said the driver in a broad Scottish accent.

Kat marvelled at the sound of such an unexpected accent.

"Scotland. Right?"

"Aye, the Shetland Islands to be exact."

"Put your window down, Ben," cried Kat, fanning her face with her hand. "I'm roasting."

Yeah, I'm sweating like a pig, but I can't let on I'm also trying to protect our driver.

As the taxi sped off, she sidled closer to Ben and took his hand. Once again, his skin burned hot and clammy. From her research role in Punta Arenas, Kat had accrued extensive knowledge of every symptom of the FIVe virus. She shivered as last night's spiel from Kurt haunted her mind. Those ill-boding words: 'a fatality rate of just over ninety-six percent.' She knew beyond doubt, both herself and Ben were infected.

Chapter Forty-Seven

The dreary grey day and her continuing head throb did nothing to lift Kat's sense of doom as the bright yellow taxi sped into the empty open landscape heading north of Punta Arenas.

After several long minutes of awkward silence, Kat struck up a conversation with the driver.

"Tell me, what made you leave the Shetland Islands …well … the top of the world, to live at the bottom of the world? I mean, it'd be the farthest possible place away wouldn't it?"

"Hehe," he giggled. "It was love, hen. Aye, it was love. For a bonnie wee lass—the daughter of one of the local fisherman here."

Kat smiled back at the twinkling blue eyes flashing in the rearview mirror.

"Aye. Now I should tell you, I do know you're both members of the research team based in the city. Still can't believe your Centre was firebombed. Your work might have rid us of this terrible virus long before now.

"Mmm, I agree. We'd have had a damn good try."

"And did you get to see the BBC news this morning?"

"No. Haven't caught up with the news today. This is the first day of our honeymoon."

He caught her eye in the mirror again and winked. "Congratulations to you both. But, aye, some sensational news this morning. An extremist group, who'd even been impersonating the CIA, has claimed responsibility for the virus. White extermination is their objective. They're even boasting of their ability to sabotage the production of vaccines. Now that tells me they were here—right here in Punta Arenas. Can you believe it?"

Kat shuddered, too gobsmacked to answer.

"But a wee bit of good news this morning too. Scientists say the virus has mutated. Aye, and because of the mutation, there's growing evidence our bodies are beginning to fight back. People are recovering from the infection."

She inched the window down even further and flopped her head back on the headrest. *He's got to be joking. I know I'm dying. And Ben's one big sweat ball.*

Kat startled from a groggy back seat doze to the sound of tussocky grass whipping at the underbody of the taxi. The little wooden cabin was right in front of them.

"Here you are, you two lovebirds, we're at the end of the road. This is your honeymoon hideaway." He leapt out and retrieved their bag.

"Come on, Ben." Kat assisted him out the door and scanned the weatherbeaten cabin.

Hmm, looks more like it was built for birds, not to observe them.

"Nice and quiet for you here," said the driver. "There's a convenience store just over there." He pointed to a gaggle of buildings in the distance. "And you're in luck," he said looking up to the sky. "The sun's come out to greet you. Anyway, I'll leave you to rest up. You're both looking pretty exhausted." He jabbered a cheery 'hehe' chuckle, then waved goodbye.

First step inside the cabin had Kat applauding Kurt's generous hospitality. The stylish décor, with its plush rugs and chintzy cushions, was a stark contrast to the building's rustic exterior.

"What a surprise, Ben. So beautifully appointed."

He let out a moan and slumped face down onto the bed. She gasped. Despite her limited knowledge of nursing, his collapse told her he'd descended into a critical stage of the viral infection.

Water, water, got to keep him hydrated. After a frantic search of the cupboards, she helped him roll onto his back and sip on a glass of water.

"You hungry, Ben?"

She gaped when he shook his head. *Ben never refuses food.*

After easing him in under the covers, she checked the pantry and refrigerator. "Wow, cupboards are full," she called out, hoping it might spark interest. "How kind of Kurt. Must have had the local shop stock up for us."

Ben didn't respond.

Kat turned on the TV. She'd been itching to verify the news scoop the taxi driver had disclosed.

"Damn it," she cried, "I've missed the BBC news."

But sure enough, although the follow-up local broadcast wasn't in English, it was obvious some major global development had broken. She gripped the remote, ogling what appeared to be an uninterrupted reel of news. Images of London's desolate streets, juxtaposed with the bustling streets of Lagos, said it all. The extended special bulletin included an interview with a person she took to be a leading scientist. However, she wasn't able to comprehend the language enough to validate the taxi drivers claim Caucasians had begun evolving immunity to the virus.

An explosive headache and a frightening dizziness forced her to switch off the TV and stagger into bed beside Ben.

Chapter Forty-Eight

A searing headache woke Kat next morning. A thin shaft of sunlight glimmered in through a gap in the curtains. She pulled at the sodden nightshirt clinging to her feverish body, then reached for Ben. The bedsheets moistened her hand, and the same unrelenting lather of sweat soaked his torso. Her eyes welled up. *We're both dying. But I don't want to be the one left to die all alone.*

"Ben, Ben, would you like something to eat?" she whispered in his ear.

"Thirsty. Water … just water," he rasped.

"Yeah, me too."

After finding two glasses, she pulled the kitchen curtain back and peered out. *What a rare day. No clouds, no wind.* The sunshine permeating the glass warmed her skin.

The beach. That's what we'll do. We'll go and enjoy the beach: the sun, the sea air. She choked with sadness. *Today will likely be our very last day together.*

In mournful silence, and with a stream of tears rolling down her cheeks, she packed their travel bag with food and water.

"C'mon, Ben, let's get you up. We're going outdoors—to the beach." She sat him on the edge of the bed for a few moments then assisted him to his feet. With a vacant stare, he placed his shaky hand in hers.

"Here, let's wrap this blanket around you Ben. I've got food and water and every blanket I could find."

"Why are we going to the beach?"

She coughed hard, in a desperate attempt to stifle a sob. *I can't tell him we're going there to die.*

There were no words. Only a gloomy hopelessness bearing down.

Despite the knifelike pain in her head, the warm spring sunshine on her face helped soothe Kat's sadness. Step by gentle step they stumbled, on through the grassy tussock, then onto the tawny brown sand. All along the way, her mind telling her this was to be their final resting place.

Ben slumped down on the blanket the minute it was spread. His eyes stared up. Glassy. Vacant. An ill-boding quivering had set in. She reached for a second blanket and wrapped it tightly around him.

Kat squirmed at the thought of mentioning death and dying. She talked all around the subject.

"You know, Ben, I'm seeing so many things in clear perspective now; like my spat with Henri—my envy of his intent to replace Levi. Then there's my obsession with body image. How petty it all seems now. All so … trifling compared to the wonder of life."

She paused, lowered her head and hugged her knees.

"By putting my career first, I've missed out on the joys of motherhood. And my parents … I so wish I'd shown them more love." She heaved a sigh. "They died so young. Right now, what more could I ask for than to end my life feeling loved by you? I've finally come to realise, love and family matter more than anything else in our lives."

There was no reply. She stared down. *Has he…?* Her heart raced in panic as she felt for his pulse. *Oh …* she exhaled, *he's fallen asleep.*

With her head in wrenching pain, and feeling drained of energy, she collapsed in a trembling heap. Her body snuggled into his. All senses and feelings drifted away.

A gentle morning breeze ruffled Kat's hair, stirring her from a deep slumber. One eye fluttered open to see the hairline of Ben's neck.

"Ben. Oh, Ben … where … where are we? The sound of the sea lapping the shore confirmed in an instant. Images from the previous day scrambled into her head. *Unless … this is all a dream?*

She raised herself on one elbow, then ran her other hand over his back. *No, I'm not dreaming. He's warm. And… No, he's not sticky hot anymore. Ben's alive! We're both alive!*

One vigorous shake was all it took to wake him. He turned over and gazed up into her eyes.

"Is that the ocean I can hear? How did we—?"

"We've survived, Ben. Our fevers have eased. The taxi driver was right. The virus did mutate. We made it."

She placed a hand on his shoulder. "How do you feel?"

"Freezing cold … and hungry."

Kat rolled out a belly laugh and smacked a kiss on his cheek. "I'm frozen too."

They sat up, wrapping themselves even tighter in their woolly blankets, then snuggled close, squinting out at the shimmering waves.

After a long silence, Ben let out a cry.

"Hey, Kat, there's something out there in the water. No … looks like there's two, and they're coming in toward the shore."

Out of the water shot two sleek bird-like figures, bouncing on their bellies in the soft sand. The birds jumped to their feet and surveyed the scene. Kat knew what they were by the distinctive black bands on their chests.

"I don't believe it, Ben. Those are Magellanic penguins. This is another miracle. They were declared extinct weeks ago."

"Well, we've survived against all odds. Why wouldn't they?"

"Just goes to prove, no matter what evil man does to ruin our beautiful planet, in the end, nature will always shine through."

Chapter Forty-Nine

As the morning sun rose higher in the sky, Kat checked her watch.

"Time we went back to the cabin, Ben. Don't know about you, but I'd love a hot drink and some toast. A hot shower too."

Ben nodded his agreement.

Shall I tell him I want to contact the hospital for an update on Sophie and the children?

Her stomach began a familiar somersaulting.

But what if it's bad news? I know, I'll phone Doctor Ariko while Ben's taking a shower.

"C'mon then, give me a hand to pack up the blankets and we'll go."

As they trudged their way back to the cabin, the earthy scent of windswept tussock grass rekindled yesterday's broodings. *I still can't believe we've survived the virus. So miraculous. And the penguins surviving too. Incredible.*

As soon as they stepped inside the cabin, Kat pointed to the bathroom. "You jump in the shower, Ben. I'll fix us something to eat."

The moment he closed the door, she grabbed her phone and contacted the hospital for an update on Sophie and the girls. Although Doctor Ariko wasn't available, she managed to converse with one of the English-speaking staff on the ward. She tugged at her hair while waiting for a nurse to come to the phone, then leaped in the air when told they were all in the recovery ward.

The minute Ben opened the bathroom door, Kat rushed to tell him what the nurse had disclosed.

"Wonderful news, Ben. Your mum, and Chloe and Zara; they're all fine now. All recovered, just like we have."

His brow furrowed in confusion.

"Don't worry, my darling," Kat threw her arms around him. "It's only your meds making you forgetful. Your mother and the girls were confined to the quarantine ward. No visitors, not even family. But now they're out. No need to worry anymore. They're all fine."

"Oh," he said, tilting his head to one side.

She watched as his brain ticked over.

"We'll go and see them. Should be there by the afternoon." Kat looked at the time. "Oh, no, I'm missing the BBC news. We can watch while I make us some breakfast."

She jumped for the remote, her attention instantly lured to the breaking news tickers sliding across the screen. The headlines made horror reading:

'Spectacular meteorite crash into East Siberian Sea.' The next caption was even more spine-chilling: 'Global concern the FIVe virus is the forerunner to a terrifying race to ethnically targeted biological warfare.'

The scene suddenly switched to commence an in-studio interview.

"Hey! She cried. "That's my friend Hugo Schuster. He's the one I sneaked the autopsy sample to. Remember? You forwarded it on to him for me."

Ben moved his mouth to reply.

"Shush. Listen. Listen!"

"Thank you for joining us, Professor Schuster. And congratulations. The world's in awe of your work in downgrading the effect of the FIVe virus to an infection that's no longer always fatal. Perhaps you'd like to give our viewers a brief overview on how you produced such a monumental achievement?"

"Basically, what we did was to engineer a competing virus. Now, I do have to admit, our modified virus is far more virulent than the FIVe virus. It had to be, to out-rival the dominance of the original. However, the good news is, the infection it causes is nowhere near as severe. I must add, we're still staggered at how rapidly our variant has become the predominant strain."

"So having achieved this incredible triumph for humanity, can we now assume a vaccine's your next goal?"

"I'm afraid not. We discovered the FIVe virus is related to the rhino virus, the scourge that causes the common cold. And like that illness, it will continue mutating. Unfortunately, that makes a preventive vaccine pretty well unachievable."

"Thank you for your time, Professor Schuster..."

"Oh, before I go, I want to take this opportunity to thank my wonderful team for their tireless dedication in neutralising the scourge that's devastated the globe. And I must add, if it hadn't been for the proactive effort of Antarctic Station team leader, Katrina Ingledew, procuring this pathogen for us, none of this would have been possible."

Kat's eyes goggled. "Wow! Did you hear that, Ben? Can you believe it? Getting recognition for the role we played."

"*We…?*"

"Yes. You were the one who arranged for the container to go to Hugo for me."

"Oh … oh yeah, so I did."

Kat slumped back into the comfort of the sofa, relieved the effect of Ben's medication had finally worn off. She pressed the off button and stared into space.

"You know what I've learned from this, Ben: always follow your intuition. I defied Henri's orders, and thanks to you, I got a second autopsy sample to Hugo. I remember thinking at the time, what the hell would The Ornithological Society do with a sample? I knew Hugo was the one who'd do what it takes. And I was right. You and I played our part in the fight for the survival of humanity."

Author Bio

A Punch from the Stars is Australian writer Graeme Goldsmith's fifth novel.